Dear Romance Reader,

Welcome to a world of breathtaking passion and never-ending romance.

Welcome to *Precious Gem Romances*.

It is our pleasure to present *Precious Gem Romances,* a wonderful new line of romance books by some of America's best-loved authors. Let these thrilling historical and contemporary romances sweep you away to far-off times and places in stories that will dazzle your senses and melt your heart.

Sparkling with joy, laughter, and love, each *Precious Gem Romance* glows with all the passion and excitement you expect from the very best in romance. Offered at a great affordable price, these books are an irresistible value—and an essential addition to your romance collection. Tender love stories you will want to read again and again, *Precious Gem Romances* are books you will treasure forever.

Look for eight fabulous new *Precious Gem Romances* each month—available only at Wal★Mart.

Lynn Brown, Publisher

SURRENDER

Lisa Plumley

Zebra Books
Kensington Publishing Corp.
http://www.zebrabooks.com

ZEBRA BOOKS are published by

Kensington Publishing Corp.
850 Third Avenue
New York, NY 10022

Copyright © 1997 by Lisa Plumley

All rights reserved. No part of this book may be reproduced in any form or by any means without the prior written consent of the Publisher, excepting brief quotes used in reviews.

If you purchased this book without a cover you should be aware that this book is stolen property. It was reported as "unsold and destroyed" to the Publisher and neither the Author nor the Publisher has received any payment for this "stripped book."

Zebra and the Z logo Reg. U.S. Pat. & TM Off.

First Printing: January, 1997
10 9 8 7 6 5 4 3 2 1

Printed in the United States of America

This one's for John—husband, lover, best friend, and the funniest man I've ever met.

. . . Do you think this happens every day?

Chapter One

It should have been a perfectly romantic evening. The lighting was soft, the music was seductive, the wine was cold. Even the weather had cooperated, in the form of an early-summer Arizona rainstorm that thrummed on the roof with a hypnotic rhythm. It was the kind of night that invited snuggling up together and forgetting the rest of the world existed.

And it would have been that kind of night, had everything gone according to Holly Aldridge's plan. Instead, things had started going downhill from the moment her boyfriend Brad came home to the cozy Craftsman-style bungalow they shared, swearing and dripping rainwater onto the foyer tile. He stripped off his wet suit jacket and, tugging at his tie, came toward her in the darkness.

"Power go out?"

"Nooo."

"Then what's with all the candles, Holly? I can hardly see a thing in here," he complained, finally whipping off his tie with a last irritable tug.

He's had a hard day, Holly thought. Be nice to him. She

patted the sofa cushion. "Mood lighting. You'll get used to it in a minute. Come sit by me."

He did, first catching hold of her feet and swinging her legs up onto the coffee table to make more room. So much for her seductive pose. She leaned into him and lay her head on the rain-dampened curve of his shoulder. "Tough day?"

Brad dropped his head back and sighed, staring up at the ceiling. "Yeah, you could say that."

"Sorry," she murmured, turning her head a little to glance up at him. Even wet and grouchy he looked good, like a glossy sort of Young Republican poster boy; not a single dark hair deviated from its prescribed course. Holly admitted to no one but herself that Brad was more skilled with mousse than she was.

She didn't want to ask about his day and be treated to an hour-long discourse on the impossibleness of practicing medicine on a bunch of patients who—as Brad put it— wouldn't recognize common sense if it fell on their heads. Once Brad got started on that, things would really go awry. So she slid a little closer and started to undo his top shirt button.

"Holly."

Buttons two and three down. He was always telling her how he was tired of making the first move. Tonight would be different. She moved lower and tackled button number four.

"Holly." This time Brad caught her wrists in his hands, as though she'd maul him if unrestrained. "Give me a little time to decompress, okay? It's been a long day."

"Okay. Sure." He let go of her wrists and pulled the ends of his shirt together again. Paradise lost. "How about a drink, then?" Holly asked brightly, filling two wineglasses with pale rosé and handing him one.

He drained his glass and set it back on the glass-topped wrought-iron coffee table with a thunk that set the tabletop ringing, completely bypassing the coasters Brad usually insisted on using. Holly frowned. Either he was very, very thirsty, or his mood was even worse than she'd thought.

She splashed more rosé into his glass, hoping it was the former. When Brad finally looked at her, fixing her with what she immediately recognized as his I'm-serious-as-hell look, Holly knew it was the latter.

"I'm sorry, Holly," he said, now looking everywhere but at her. "Really sorry. But I just can't do this anymore. You and me . . . it's not working; things just aren't right for me."

Cold trickled down her spine. Of course things were right. She'd planned everything, right down to his favorite ratatouille simmering on the stove, down to the CDs she'd programmed on the stereo, down to the perfume the tastefully made-up woman at the Esteé Lauder counter had assured Holly was "irresistible, dear." She wouldn't have gone to such trouble for a doomed relationship, would she?

"What do you mean?" Her voice sounded faraway, broken. She finished off her wine for fortification and glanced over at him. Any second now he'd come out with a cliché like, "I need some space, that's all," and she'd nod her head wisely and tell him she'd been thinking exactly the same thing about herself, wasn't that funny, ha ha. And then she'd brain him with the wine bottle and boot him out into the rain.

"I—" he spread out his arms in a choreographed sort of helpless gesture, careful not to actually touch her. "I've got to get away for a while, do some thinking. I guess I just need some space, that's all."

Oh, God. "Brad, I—" Her lower lip trembled, her chin wobbled. She would not cry, she wouldn't. Holly poured more rosé and gulped it down. "I . . . that's funny, 'cause I was just thinking the same thing," Holly croaked. It lacked a certain conviction, but it was the best she could do under the circumstances.

He lay both hands on his thighs and pushed up from the sofa. "I knew you'd understand," he said, ruffling her hair as he passed by. So much for her carefully-arranged, seductive hairstyle.

"Mmmm . . . what's that great smell?" he went on, looking brisk and assured. *Whew,* his expression said, *Glad that's over with!* Brad hated scenes. "Mind if I eat before I pack up? I'm starving."

"It's ratatouille," she replied numbly. "Help yourself."

"Help yourself? You actually said to him, 'Gee, Brad, help yourself'? Oh, Holly."

Feeling miserable, Holly slumped down further into her kitchen banquette's corner, resting her cheek against its soft yellow upholstery.

"Quit shaking your head at me, Clarissa. Come on, it wasn't as dumb as it sounds. It just popped out. I couldn't help it."

"Uh-huh."

"It was supposed to sound cosmopolitan. 'Sure, darling—of course we can still be friends,' something like that. You know. And I didn't say gee, either," Holly added indignantly. "God, you're supposed to be my friend! What am I supposed to do now?"

Clarissa gave her a sympathetic look. "Sorry. I didn't realize Brad the Bad meant so much to you."

"Ha, ha." With a sigh Holly wrapped one arm around her upraised knees and reached for her cup of cappuccino—courtesy of the espresso machine Brad had left behind. She'd need to drink a gallon of the stuff to feel awake after what she'd been through. Maybe two gallons. In fact, maybe she should just skip a step and gnaw on the coffee beans. The wine she'd drunk last night had been a mistake, especially when followed by a can of Brad's orphaned beer and a vodka chaser. She didn't know what she'd been thinking.

"I feel like such an idiot. I didn't even see it coming. How could I be so blind?"

"You weren't blind, he was stupid," Clarissa replied loyally. "What kind of cheesy line is that anyway? 'Babe'—" she flipped her long pale hair over her shoulders and pantomimed a Brad-like stance, both hands on her hips with her chest thrust forward, " '—I need my space.' Didn't that line go out about the same time lava lamps did?"

Holly managed a brief smile. Clarissa was right—Brad's reasons for ending their relationship were weak, but the fact of the matter was, he didn't really need an excuse. He only needed to be gone for it to be over, and he was. She was all alone.

Lord, she sounded pathetic. Poor me. Pity party. Get a grip already, Holly commanded herself. You've got a good job, good friends, a good life. Where's your self-respect?

"Anyway, I have a plan," she said aloud.

Clarissa grinned. "Somehow, I thought you would."

"What's funny? In case you haven't noticed, this could be considered a tragic moment in my life, here." She picked up a pen and opened her day-planner, trying to ignore her friend's skeptical expression. "Okay. Brad and I have been together for a little over a year now. No problems until last night."

"Really? That's amazing."

"You're turning into a cynic."

Clarissa gathered up both coffee cups and carried them to the sink. "No, really—" prompted by Holly's meaningful glance at the brown-ringed porcelain cups, she turned on the tap and gave each cup a cursory swish "—didn't the two of you ever argue? About anything?"

"Nope."

"Hmmph." Clarissa grabbed a cinnamon-raisin bagel from the basket on the kitchen table and settled back on the other banquette, picking out the raisins with her long red manicured fingernails. She popped a raisin in her mouth, then another. "I've got to be honest here, Holly-Berry. That's abnormal."

"It's true," Holly insisted, printing one last note into her day-planner. "Maybe we didn't argue because we were so well suited for each other."

"Well suited? Did we warp back into the Dark Ages when I wasn't looking? What are you talking about, well suited? I don't think arranged marriages are happening anymore."

"Very funny." Ticking off each similarity on her fingers,

Holly said, "Brad and I are the same age. We went to the same schools. Both of us grew up here. We've got the same goals—"

"Career, career, and . . . career?" Clarissa suggested.

"No, I mean life goals. Like we both want a family." Or at least Brad hadn't actively discouraged her on those few occasions when she'd talked about having children together someday. Holly tilted her head sideways, thinking. There had to be more things they had in common. "We're even the same height," she announced triumphantly.

Twirling the remains of her bagel on one finger, Clarissa said, "Really? I always thought Brad was taller than you."

"I slouched," Holly admitted. They both grinned. Meanly. "But all the right elements were there, and I'm not just going to let this pass me by. I'm practically thirty—"

"Nearly dead," Clarissa broke in, nodding and grinning.

"—And it's time I settled down."

Clarissa shook her head. "You've got to be the most settled-down person I know. You've got a retirement plan. You've got coordinated bath towels, for crying out loud. Even my mother doesn't have towels that all match."

Holly's towels did match. Down to the washcloths they were all a suitably masculine burgundy color, the only one she and Brad had both liked. "There's more to life than decorating," Holly said, ignoring Clarissa's raised eyebrows. "Besides, Brad and I had a good relationship. Maybe we were taking each other for granted, maybe some of the spark went out of things, but I think we had something worth saving," she insisted.

Clarissa looked doubtful. Well, let her, Holly thought rebelliously. It wasn't *Clarissa's* love life that had taken a nosedive. Clarissa had been happily married for three years now; she could afford to take the high moral ground.

Squinting at the notes she'd penned neatly into her day-planner, Holly said, "Anyway, my theory is what we've got here is a fear of commitment. I think Brad and I just got so close it scared him."

"I guess so. Maybe."

"Your enthusiasm is too much for me," Holly muttered wryly. She gathered her convictions again. "It's like I said. Maybe Brad and I were just taking each other for granted and we got caught in a rut, or something," she explained, hoping her reasoning sounded more convincing to Clarissa than it suddenly did to her.

Last night, lying in bed alone, it had all made perfect sense. Unfortunately, Holly really hadn't come up with any better interpretations since then. Her feelings, her love life, her pride were at stake; her life didn't *feel* like it was supposed to anymore, and Holly couldn't bear to sit back and do nothing at all about it.

"I mean, Brad didn't actually say we were through, not in so many words . . ."

Clarissa gaped at her. "Oh, jeez, tell me you don't mean what I think you mean—"

Holly nodded, smiling down with renewed hope at the notes she'd made. Her Plan. She felt a little better already, just looking at it. "You guessed it. I'm going to win Brad back. I've already got it all planned out. And I'll need your help to do it."

Clarissa smacked her palm against her forehead. "Lord help us," she cried. "That's just what I was afraid of."

Sam McKenzie had always loved the last day of school. His final act as a student each year had been to haul everything out of his locker and cram it into a backpack for the trip home—where it would sit, untouched, until September. Now, as the college English professor he'd become, things weren't much different.

Sure, now it was his desk he emptied out, and his things were going into a battered old box instead of a backpack, but as he wedged the last file folder beneath his weighty American Literature text, Sam doubted he'd crack a book again before autumn rolled around. No books, no suits, no ties—he planned to pack up his razor, too, and really relax. It was a good feeling.

Not even the prospect of working for his Dad's construction company all summer was enough to dampen his spirits. A guy had to eat, after all. It was worth the inevitable get-a-haircut-and-get-a-real-man's-job lecture from his father that was the price of admission. In a way, it was Sam's own personal penance for not going into the family business.

"Okay, I'm outta here," he said, hefting the box in his arms. Malcolm Jeffries, campus advisor for returning students and Sam's office-mate for the past semester, sniffed vaguely, but didn't bother to look up. He'd made his disapproval of what he called Sam's unorthodox teaching methods plain from the start, and Malcolm was nothing if not unvarying in his opinions. It had made for a bumpy partnership.

Today, not even Malcolm's standardized-test-approach to life could get to Sam. "Hey, have a good summer," he told Malcolm with a grin. "See you next fall."

The grunt he received in response could've meant anything. Optimistically decoding the sound as, "You, too," Sam turned toward the door and all but ran into one of his students, Jillian Hall.

Affectionately known to the student body as Jiggly Jillie, Jillie lived up to her nickname and then some. Even when standing still, like she was now, Jillie's blond froth of permed curls, combined with the twirl of her summery short skirt and the sway of her breasts beneath her T-shirt, somehow gave the impression of perpetual motion. It was quite a phenomenon.

"Professor McKenzie, I'm so glad you're here," she said, a little breathlessly. "I wanted to talk to you about my research paper."

She was watching him so earnestly, with such intensity, it looked as though her wide blue eyes might cross at any second. Sam shoved all jiggly thoughts aside and tried to assume a more professorial demeanor. "Sure, Jillie. What's on your mind?"

"Well, there must've been some kinda mistake on my research paper. I can't have gotten a D," she wailed, holding up a stack of typed pages for him to see. "If I don't do better than that in this class, my financial aid is history!"

Sam took the papers she was waving at him. He recognized them all right; it had taken him four aspirin and several cups of coffee to finish reading and grading those few pages of freshman composition.

"What happened to your paper on the use of lab animals in cosmetics testing—the one you outlined for me?" Sam asked gently. "You had some very good ideas for that; it could've been a good position paper, like we discussed in class."

Jillie ducked her head and thrust her lower lip forward. The gesture would've looked more at home on a four-year-old than the twenty-four-year-old single mother of two toddlers Sam knew her to be.

"I thought you'd like this better," she told him, fiddling uncomfortably with her pink-polished fingernails. "It's more serious. I thought you'd be impressed."

"Hearing your own ideas would impress me the most. The best papers come when you really care about your subject, Jillie. Maybe I'm wrong, but I'm not sure global warming is something near and dear to your heart."

Sam glanced meaningfully at her paper. Touching her shoulder, he added, "Environmentalism is a worthy subject, sure, but I don't think you had time to research this properly, and—"

Her eyes filled with tears. "You're just like Mr. Jeffries!" she accused, darting a narrow-eyed glance at Sam's officemate. "He doesn't think I belong in college. Him and all those tests he does say I was meant to be a cosmetologist and that's what I ought to stay." Her gaze swung around to Sam again, her eyes red-rimmed and teary. "You're no better, are you? You two don't want people like me here at all."

Sam shook his head. Hell, *he* was people like Jillie, a guy who'd spent high school screwing around and the years afterward getting into one scrape after another. He was twenty-three before he finally worked up the guts to walk into the college admissions office, and even then he'd half-expected to get laughed out of the place. He remembered what it was like to sweat over the placement tests, the first few papers, the exams.

Besides, he'd rather die than be lumped into the same tight-assed category as Malcolm Jeffries.

"Tell you what," Sam said thoughtfully, nodding toward his box of books and files. "My final grade sheet is still in there. I've got to drop it off by five o'clock, but I think I could see my way clear to writing in a C for your final grade—"

"Really?" Jillie asked, sniffling.

Sam nodded.

"Oh, professor—you don't know what this means to me!" She hugged herself, bobbing a little in a happy kind of jig.

"Hold on," he said sternly, one hand upraised. "There's a catch. I want you to rewrite your paper. You can redo global warming—and put some hard research into it this time—but it would be a shame to waste all the work you've already put into your cosmetics testing idea."

Jillie stopped jiggling. She glanced sideways, biting her lower lip pensively. "Oh, I guess you're right. Okay."

"I know I'm right." Shuffling through his files, Sam tore off a slip of paper and wrote his address on it. "You've got my phone number—call me if you get stuck. Otherwise—" he handed Jillie the paper "—you can drop off your paper to me no later than Friday. I'm leaving town after that."

She clutched the scrap of paper like a lifeline. "Thanks, thank you so much. You'll have it by Friday, I promise," she enthused, her smile widening as she turned to go. Sam picked up his box again, watching her. Halfway down the hall, Jillie paused and, with a wave, called, "You won't regret this, professor! Thanks!"

Sam wanted to believe she was right. Something warned him otherwise; some niggling doubt in the back of his mind told him he might regret his decision very much. Then he realized it wasn't intuition at all. It was the sight of Malcolm Jeffries' gloating face peering at him through his open office door.

"I'll have your butt in a sling for this, McKenzie," his office-mate said with a sneer. "I always knew you were a lousy teacher, and now I've got proof. You just wait. Your little arrangement with Jiggly is going to blow up in your face like your worst nightmare."

Sam glanced over at him, making a little tsk-tsk sound. "Gotta watch those mixed metaphors, Malcolm," he said, and then he was off to enjoy the summer.

Two days after the romantic dinner that wasn't, Holly's conviction that she and Brad belonged together hadn't wavered. This was despite a minor setback that occurred when she came home to find Brad sneaking out of the house, his arms laden with the cappuccino maker and both stereo speakers.

"Hey, those are mine!" She hurried up the front walk as fast as her two-inch heels and double burden of briefcase and gym bag would allow, and met Brad just outside the front door.

"Huh?" He craned his neck sideways and peered at her through his glasses in that adorably owlish way he had. His eyes looked greener than ever, she noticed. Holly steeled her resolve. However appealing he might look, she wasn't about to let him demolish their stereo system, even for the short time they were going to be apart.

"Oh, it's just you, Holly," Brad said, looking surprised. "I, uh . . . didn't think you'd be home yet."

She tapped the top of the nearest speaker. Her new manicure—one of Clarissa's contributions to The Plan—gleamed richly in the sunlight. Brad hated sloppy-looking women. "These are mine, remember?"

"The *stereo* is yours, Holly. These speakers belong to me," he reminded her as he headed down the sidewalk toward his car. Holly dumped her briefcase and gym bag on the welcome mat and followed him.

"You blew your tiny little speakers the day after we moved in together, remember?" he added.

"Oh, yeah." Some passing spiteful impulse made her lean against the door of his red BMW while she watched him load up his things. He slammed the trunk shut, noticed she was still there, and yanked her away from the car. He even looked cute when he scowled. "Christ, Holly—I just waxed it."

I'll bet, she thought. "Ooops," she said aloud. The damn car got more stroking than she ever had, it occurred to her.

"What're you doing here, anyway?" he asked accusingly, glancing at his watch. "It's only ... oh. You're right on time, I guess. I didn't realize it had gotten so late already."

Holly propped her hands on her hips, turning her body toward him in a friendly way so the neighbors wouldn't guess they were anything less than blissfully happy together. Temporarily. "What are you talking about?"

"Well, it's 6:30, isn't it?" Brad replied, rummaging around in his pants pocket and coming up with his car keys a few seconds later. Holly could tell from his expression this cryptic explanation was supposed to mean something to her, but for the life of her she couldn't figure out what. "So what?"

To his credit, he looked almost sorry to have brought up the whole subject. "So you're a little predictable, that's what. You leave work at 5:15 every weekday. Afterwards you go to the gym for an hour—if it's Monday, Wednesday, or Friday—then home. They could set clocks by you, you're so unspontaneous."

"I am not!" Holly protested, but he was warming to his subject now, she could tell. He nodded his head at the neatly folded paper bag sticking out of her gym bag. "Your lunch, right?" She nodded. "I'll bet it was a turkey sandwich on wheat," he began.

"This is dumb."

"—With brown mustard, lettuce on the side," Brad recited. "Tomato juice to drink, with a bendy straw. And a green apple."

"It was a red apple," Holly shot back.

"I'm leaving." He opened the car door, slid inside, and revved the engine. She rapped on the window.

He pressed the button that rolled it down. "Let's not make this any harder than it has to be," Brad said. "I'm not trying to hurt you, you know. I just can't deal with all this right now. I told you—I need some space."

Was it just her, or was his regretful expression a little at odds with the way he kept revving the car's engine, as though impatient to be gone?

"Sure." Predictable, he'd said. Unspontaneous. "I understand." When she got done with her Plan, Brad wouldn't know what hit him. "I just wanted to tell you, I need your house keys back."

He grinned. Then he laughed. She felt like kicking him.

"What for?" he asked, twisting his key ring to release his set of house keys. He dropped them, warm from his fingers, into her palm. "You've found another roommate already?"

Predict this, Holly thought. "As a matter of fact, I have. And *he's* moving in this weekend. See ya."

Nothing like a little competition to enliven the game, she told herself. Didn't every man want what he couldn't have? Tempting as it was, she didn't even linger to savor the sight of Brad's mouth hanging open in surprise. She couldn't—she had to get busy finding that new roommate.

"I told you, I'm not interested in having a roommate." Easing his pickup truck into the early-morning traffic that streamed into town, Sam McKenzie looked away from the road long enough to be sure his cousin Clarissa was listening to him. She wasn't. Oh, she was nodding her head, all right, but he'd known Clarissa since they were both four feet tall—long enough to realize that with her, a nod didn't necessarily indicate agreement. Sam sighed.

"I'm only in town for the summer, then I'm back to the city. I'm sure your friend Holly is terrific, but I'm not in the market for a roommate. I like to live alone."

Beside him across the wide bench seat, Clarissa snorted. "Is that why you're staying with your folks, because you like to be alone? You know I love you like a brother, Sam, but I've got to be honest, here. That's truly pathetic."

"Don't hold back," he said with a wry grin, "tell me what you really think." She hit him in the shoulder, a punch probably aimed at his upper arm, but sent awry by the bouncing of his old truck. "Ouch! Does David know he's married to such a bruiser?"

"My husband doesn't give me any reason to punch him," Clarissa returned archly. "Unlike my knot-headed cousin. Besides, I barely touched you." She twisted in the seat, half-crushing the white bakery bag of donuts beside her. Sam snatched it out of the way and dropped the sack into a safer spot atop the dashboard.

He turned his attention to the road again, automatically scanning the streets and buildings around them. Everything looked the same as it ever did in Saguaro Vista, the same as it had since he was a kid steering a bike down Main Street instead of his pickup. The old adobe buildings looked a little more worn, and now there were strip malls sprouting up like weeds at the edges of town, but all in all it was nice to come back to. Comforting.

His mouthy cousin was anything but.

"Anyway, the only time you're alone is when you're between girlfriends," she was saying, sounding so primly sure of herself he couldn't stand it.

"I've never lived with any of them, either," he protested, but Clarissa overrode him, giving Sam a look that allowed no argument.

"I'm not asking you to marry Holly, for god's sake! She's got a boyfriend she's dead-set on already, though I can't imagine why."

Clarissa gazed out the passenger-side window, the very picture of nonchalance. Sam didn't buy her act for a minute. This roommate thing mattered a lot to her, or she wouldn't have been nagging him about it for the past two days.

"This boyfriend doesn't object to her having a male

roommate?" Either the guy was very, very sure of himself—and her—or he was just plain stupid.

"Well, technically they're separated." She must have sensed him weakening, because Clarissa smiled and moved in for the kill. "Come on, do it as a favor to me, if nothing else. It wouldn't hurt you to think of somebody besides yourself for a change."

Sam jerked the truck to a stop in the mesquite-shaded parking lot of the Downtown Grill and glared at her. "Just what the hell is that supposed to mean?"

Not in the least threatened, Clarissa snapped open her seat belt and pulled up the door handle. The door creaked open, scattering dust in its wake. "Look. I just want the people I care about to be happy, that's all," she said quietly. "If your answer's still no after you meet Holly, then I'll drop the whole thing, okay?"

Sam stared at her suspiciously. Maybe it was because she'd worn him down, maybe it was because he wanted to prove he wasn't the self-centered jerk she'd all-but accused him of being, maybe it was because he was starving and just wanted their conversation to end; whatever the reason, he nodded his head.

"Okay," he said finally. "I'll meet your damn friend."

"Great!"

Clarissa hopped out of the truck and came around to Sam's side to meet him. Apparently undaunted despite the fact he'd used his best, most grumbly, feet-dragging tone, she grabbed his arm and swept him along beside her toward the double glass doors of the Downtown Grill.

"There's Holly's car right over there," she said, her wave indicating a little white MG convertible parked a few feet away. "She must be inside waiting for us right now."

Sam stopped walking. "Did it never occur to you I might say no?"

"Nah," Clarissa said, stepping back to let him open the door for her and giving him a self-satisfied smile. "I usually get what I want."

With an answering grin, Sam ushered her through the door. "Must run in the family," he said. "So do I."

Chapter Two

All right, maybe it was just a *teensy* bit juvenile to try and make Brad jealous, Holly admitted to herself as she sat alone in a cracked leather booth at the Downtown Grill waiting for Clarissa to meet her for breakfast. Granted, she'd been provoked into her boast about a roommate she didn't have yet. And her decision had certainly been a spontaneous one, which was some consolation to her bruised ego. Still, she was almost starting to regret the way those words had just popped out of her mouth.

"Hey, Holly!" The sound of Clarissa's voice, loud enough even to carry over the din of the restaurant, yanked her out of her worries. Glancing up, Holly saw her friend wending nearer between the rows of customer-filled booths.

She wasn't alone; there was a man with her. Tall and shaggy-haired, dressed in paint-splattered Levis, a white T-shirt, and a blue chambray overshirt, he somehow managed to look both friendly and slightly disreputable at the same time. He didn't look familiar, but then Holly had been working such long hours she'd fallen out of touch with many of the people in town.

"I've solved your roommate problem!" Clarissa announced gaily when she'd reached the table. She waved one arm in the general direction of the man beside her. "Holly Aldridge, meet Samuel McKenzie."

"Sam," he corrected. "Clarissa's told me all about you."

His smile was so inviting that, despite her better judgement, Holly smiled back at him.

"I hope everything she said was good," Holly said, accepting the handshake he offered. His palm was callused but clean, and big, like the rest of him. Holly felt his gaze sweep over her, from the collar of her black suit-jacket downward and back again. His appreciative expression took her by surprise. How long had it been since Brad had looked at her like that, since any man had looked at her like that?

Too long.

"Every bit of it was good," he assured her. "It's nice to meet you." He sounded like he meant it. Holly gave herself a mental shake and withdrew her hand, watching as they settled themselves into the opposite side of the booth.

This was the answer to her roommate problem? He was really very attractive, in a relaxed, just-rolled-out-of-bed sort of way, but by the looks of him Holly doubted Sam McKenzie even had a job, much less the means to pay half her mortgage payment each month. She slid the hot water and tea she'd already ordered for Clarissa over to her friend, along with a curious glance.

Clarissa ignored Holly's questioning look. Uncharacteristically, she remained absolutely silent as she fussed with her tea. In fact, Holly noticed, her lips were pressed tightly together, like a child "zipping her lips" to keep a secret. Something was definitely up.

"Clarissa says you're looking for a roommate," Sam said, filling the silence at their table. He turned over the thick white porcelain cup in front of him and settled it into its saucer. Like magic a pink-skirted waitress appeared and filled it with coffee. Holly wondered absently if Sam got service like that every place he went, and decided he probably did.

"Yes, I am. My last roommate just moved out,"—why had she called Brad her roommate?—"and I've been looking for someone to, er, replace him."

Sam nodded. Clarissa snickered and dunked a tea bag in and out of her cup with far more interest than the Earl Grey required. She looked like the cat who ate the canary. Holly frowned.

"Is it a house or an apartment?" Sam asked.

As though pulled by his voice, she looked at him again. He had nice eyes, too—clear blue beneath a pile of messy, shoulder-length, sandy-colored hair. Guitar-player hair, Holly thought; I can't believe it.

"It's a house. One of those old bungalows downtown," she replied. Why wasn't Clarissa saying anything?

"Those Craftsman-style bungalows near Spring Street?"

"Why, yes," she replied, surprised he was familiar with the architectural movement that had spawned row after row of houses downtown in the first decades of the century. Hers was one of the few examples of the style that remained unchanged; many had been demolished to make way for shops and newer stucco houses.

"Those are great houses," he was saying. "Ahead of their time, I think. It's too bad there are so few left now."

"Holly's renovating hers," Clarissa chimed in. "It's going to be beautiful."

"Tell me about it," Sam said, handing her a leather-bound copy of the Downtown Grill's menu as though the motion was the most natural thing in the world. As though they'd shared meals together forever.

Holly blinked. *Get real*, she ordered herself, pushing that wild thought out of her mind. She couldn't really be interested in him, could she? Muscle-bound laborers had never been her type. She wanted a man with a future, a man with intelligence and wit, a man who thought beyond his next conquest . . . a man like Brad.

Besides, a guy like Sam probably favored leggy blondes in spandex, not sensible redheads in Chanel knockoff business suits. Holly set down the menu without opening it. "I'm still looking for a contractor to handle the bulk of the renovation," she said evenly. "There are parts I can do myself, but I'd like to get an expert's opinion, too."

Sam raised an eyebrow at Clarissa, giving her an odd look. "What a coincidence," he remarked. To Holly, he said, "I know a little about whole-house renovation. I'd love to have a look at it sometime."

"Sure."

The waitress, pen and pad in hand, chose that moment to take their order. Holly declined anything but her coffee; Clarissa and Sam both ordered plates of the Grill's special pecan pancakes, his with a double side of bacon. Scooping up their menus, the waitress went on her gum-snapping way toward the restaurant's kitchen.

"Sam's doing some work for my uncle's construction company over the summer," Clarissa explained.

"I see." At least this potential roommate Clarissa had found for her was employed, Holly thought. "Do you like it?" she asked politely.

"I like the work. It's absorbing, doing a job just right, seeing a vision come to life. Done well, renovation is demanding, but creative." Sam's eyes met hers. "Besides," he said slowly, "I'm very good with my hands."

Holly's gaze flew to his hands. Her mouth went dry. Had he meant to say those words that way, so . . . so loaded with erotic meaning? Surely it was only her imagination.

He leaned back against the booth again, his shoulders nearly reaching the top of it. "How about tonight? Say, 6:30?"

"Tonight?" For a few confused seconds, Holly actually thought he was proposing some sort of illicit meeting, some personal demonstration of those hands' promised abilities. One glance at Sam dispelled that illusion, however. He was asking to see her house, nothing more.

Before she could reply, Clarissa said, "You sound just like your dad, Sam. Straight down to business." Turning to Holly, she added, "My Uncle Joe has got to be the most single-minded guy in town."

How she was supposed to react to *that* statement, Holly had no idea. Then the significance of Clarissa's words dawned on her. Sam McKenzie was Clarissa's "little cousin Sam." Funny how she'd never mentioned that in this case, at least, little meant he was a couple of years younger. Sam was most definitely not the Little League-sized relative Holly had always assumed him to be. She glared at Clarissa and silently mouthed, "I'll get you for this."

With feigned innocence, Clarissa raised her eyebrows. Who, me? her expression asked. Aloud, she said, "That's why I thought Sam would make such a perfect roommate for you, Holly. He's dependable,"—Holly couldn't decipher the look that passed between the two cousins—"great with old houses, and he'll only be in town for the next three months."

"Three months?" Holly asked.

"Just until next semester starts," Sam explained, going on to describe his September-through-May work as an English professor at the university in Tucson. Holly was surprised—they sure hadn't had professors like Sam when *she* was a student at the University of Arizona. She bet his students loved him.

A few minutes later the waitress slid two enormous plates of pecan pancakes onto the table, followed by an aromatic pile of bacon she set in front of Sam, along with the bill. Holly's stomach rumbled as the sugary smell of maple syrup reached her.

Sam swallowed a bite of pancake, speared another with his fork, and held it out to her. "Want a bite?"

She couldn't imagine doing anything so intimate as eating from his fork, Sam guiding the bit of food into her mouth as Clarissa and the whole world looked on. Brad would've been appalled by the very idea, had she ever suggested it to him.

With Sam on the other end of the fork, though, the idea had a new appeal. Some small, hidden part of her *wanted* to try it, urged her to try it. Holly considered it as, spellbound, she watched an amber drop of maple syrup gather on the tip of his fork tines, tremble, then drip slowly to join the butter and syrup puddle on Sam's plate.

Oh, boy—she was really losing it.

Sam raised his eyebrows. "It's delicious—do you want to try some?"

Holly shook her head. "Um, no—I already ate breakfast," she managed to say. Lord, she'd never been skilled at small talk, but this was ridiculous.

"Anyway, as I was saying, Holly, wouldn't it be perfect if Sam moved in with you? I mean, as your roommate, of course," Clarissa said with a wicked grin. "Aren't you expecting your—ah, former roommate?—to move back in at the end of the summer anyway?"

She meant Brad, naturally. "Maybe even sooner," Holly felt compelled to say. "In fact, I'm starting to rethink this whole idea of finding a temporary roommate altogether."

Clarissa looked stricken. "But that's not what you *planned*," she said. "I think Sam here would really help with your *Plan*, don't you?" Her emphasis on the word plan left little doubt what she was referring to—Holly's plan to win back Brad. A broad wink or two would've made their resemblance to Lucy and Ethel complete.

Sam cleared his throat. They both looked at him. "Isn't that up to Holly?" he asked mildly.

Holly liked him better already. She smiled. "Sam's right," she said, gathering up her day planner, purse, sunglasses, and car keys. "And I'm going to be late for work if I don't get out of here."

"It's Memorial Day! You're not taking the day off?" Clarissa asked, looking appalled.

"And leave my in box full of work?" Holly shook her head. The office was always quietest on holidays and weekends—she'd get tons of work done, and be that much further ahead by tomorrow.

"Oh, right—what was I thinking?" Clarissa smacked her forehead with the heel of her hand, then frowned. "You probably only put in *sixty* hours last week, huh?"

Okay, so Holly would be the first to admit she was ambitious. What was wrong with that? There'd been a time when Clarissa had put in just as much overtime as Holly did. They'd become friends over deli-delivered sandwiches, eaten long past five o'clock in one of their adjoining office cubicles. Once she'd married David, Clarissa had decided she was happy where she was, but Holly still yearned for an office of her own and the title that went with it.

"You've got to stop and smell the roses sometime, you know," Clarissa warned. "Life's passing you by."

"There's no need to be so dire," Holly said, feeling exasperated. "Once I make senior-level accountant, I'll have plenty of time to stop and smell the roses."

Clarissa's expression said she'd believe *that* when she saw it. Holly sighed and let go of their old argument. She couldn't explain what drove her to work more and more hours, to achieve yet another of her ever-multiplying goals. She only knew her efforts hadn't quite measured up. Not yet.

"We're headed out to the lake later," Sam said, calling her back to their conversation. "Clarissa and David and I—sure you don't want to come? It would be great to have you."

The invitation was tempting, especially when accompanied by Sam's seductive grin. "Come on," he coaxed, his voice lowering, "it'll be fun."

He nodded toward the door, as though they'd pick up right there and head outside, just for the fun of it. Holly could picture it: a cool swim, the hot, sun-warmed sand . . . her and Sam.

You'll never get that promotion that way, a voice inside her whispered. Shut up, she thought. But the tide was turned.

"I can't. I'm sorry," Holly said. "Thanks for the invitation, though. You guys have fun."

She glanced at her watch. "Now I really am late. Do you still want to see the house tonight?"

Sam nodded. "I'd love to."

Holly whipped open her day planner. "Is six-thirty okay with you?" she asked.

"I'll be there with bells on," Sam answered. His words called to mind a very interesting image, one Holly refused to contemplate beyond a few seconds. Almost as though he'd guessed what she'd been thinking, Sam added with a wink, "It's been a pleasure meeting you, Holly."

She fled before he could guess anything more incriminating.

At 6:25 that evening, Sam McKenzie pulled his pickup truck up in front of Holly's white-framed house at the address Clarissa had given him. The porch light was on, and lamplight shone through both of the curtained front windows. It looked welcoming. Heading up the walk, juggling the things he'd brought, he surveyed the house with approval. It was sturdy, if a little run-down, and it had a character newer houses typically lacked.

Pink geraniums crowded together in the built-in stone planters that flanked the porch steps and filled the air with their spicy scent. The porch itself was clean-swept, adorned with only a welcome mat and a white wood swing that swayed in the breeze. The loud clunk of his boots on the floorboards must have announced his arrival, because just as Sam touched the doorbell, Holly opened the door.

"Hi! You're here." She sounded surprised. He peered through the aluminum screened door, trying to gauge her reaction. With the light behind her, though, her face was cast into shadow.

"Did you think I wouldn't show?"

"I, ummm . . . well, I guess not," she replied, pushing the door open to let him in. "I mean, I didn't think you *wouldn't.*" Holly smiled and rolled her eyes. "That is, you said you would, and I can't imagine anybody who's related to Clarissa saying anything they didn't mean. It must be in the bloodline or something."

He laughed as he moved past her into the house. He'd say one thing for Holly; she definitely had his cousin pegged.

"We're not generally known to be hesitant about things," Sam agreed. One of those things he wasn't hesitant about was Holly. From the moment he'd touched her in the restaurant he'd felt something between them, something hot and intriguing and inevitable. It was that feeling, more than mere architectural curiosity, that had brought him to her house.

Sam turned to face her and saw she was looking at the flat white box in his hand. Nodding at it, Holly sniffed suspiciously at the savory aroma rising from it. "What's that?"

"I brought dinner," he replied, brandishing the box that was rapidly heating his left hand. "Pizza, from Angelo's." He handed over the bottle of red wine he'd brought. "And something to drink. I hope you haven't eaten already."

"No—in fact, I just got home from work," Holly told him, motioning with the bottle for Sam to follow her through the wood-framed archway to the kitchen. He did.

"I didn't think I'd be at the office as long as I was," she went on, setting the wine atop the counter, then opening the cupboard and pulling out a pair of plates. "Once I get going, I lose track of time, sometimes."

With a shy smile she reached for the pizza box he'd been balancing on one hand and slid it gracefully onto the countertop. "I was half-afraid you'd get here before I did."

"You're an accountant?" Sam asked, remembering their conversation at the Grill earlier.

"Officially, I'm a controller," Holly replied, "but that's just a fancy word for it. I work for the county, like Clarissa."

She went on to describe the people the agency served, and the various functions of her office, with an enthusiasm Sam might have found unbelievable coming from anyone else. Somehow, it seemed very real coming from Holly. Her words came faster, keeping tempo with her double-speed gestures. Holly talked about depreciation and budgets with the same zeal his buddies reserved for, say, strip poker or professional football.

She paused. "Why are you smiling like that?"

Sam flipped open the pizza box, stalling for time. "This looks great, doesn't it?" he offered. Holly's inquisitive expression never wavered. He wasn't going to get off the hook that easily.

"You're lucky to have work you love," Sam said, realizing only as he said it how true those words were. "Even if it is something like *accounting*," he added with a mock shudder.

"Hey!" Holly protested. "I happen to be very good at what I do."

"I believe you," he assured her. She looked skeptical. Sam went on anyway. "Not everybody is lucky enough to spend their days doing something they love."

She turned her back to the counter and leaned against

it, listening, her palms propped on the edge for balance. "Are you?"

He'd walked right into that one. "Until recently, no," Sam answered. "Now I am."

He lifted a wedge of pizza from the box and transferred it to a plate, then handed it to Holly. She was watching him intently.

"But your teaching helps people," she said. "Do you think that makes a difference?"

Holly took a bite of pizza, then set the plate down again and moved a little closer. Her eyes were green, Sam noticed, green as new spring grass. She expected an answer; he knew it.

Sam wanted to give her one. But standing there so close, close enough to smell the faint muskiness of her perfume, thoughts of work and career planning were the furthest things from his mind.

She seemed different tonight. Why, he couldn't tell for sure. It wasn't her clothes—they were the same kind of lady-lawyer stuff she'd been wearing in the restaurant earlier—a pair of ordinary khaki pants and a plain white shirt. So why was he imagining himself unbuttoning those buttons, revealing the woman underneath? Why was he wondering what Holly would do if he leaned over and kissed her, if he pinned her against the countertop and lost himself in her?

"Sam?"

He'd forgotten what they'd been talking about. Some smooth talker he was, Sam thought. He scrambled for the topic at hand.

"Yeah, I think helping people makes a difference. And for me it was a lot of little things that added up to a job I loved. I didn't plan it that way. Once I'd taken the first step, the rest just followed."

He lifted a slice of pizza for himself, not bothering with a plate, and took a bite. Beneath the toppings, the double cheese and sauce were still hot. Perfect. Sam closed his eyes and savored the first bite. When he opened them again, Holly's curious green-eyed gaze was still focused on him.

"You're the lucky one," she said. "I don't think anything's ever happened to me that I didn't have to work for." She laughed a little and reached for the wine bottle, pouring them each a glass. "Don't get me wrong, for the most part I've been successful. But I can't imagine just leaving things to chance like that, waiting to see what comes."

"Why not? Sometimes what comes along is exactly what you've been looking for."

Holly shook her head. "I just can't see it."

Sam wondered what kind of failure she'd come up against, what it was that had wrecked her "mostly successful" planning. Whatever it was, it had made her a woman afraid to travel without a road map at her side. He didn't know how to explain joyriding to a woman like that.

"You must have pretty detailed plans for your house renovation, then," he remarked, glancing around the kitchen. A spacious, open-planned room, it was trimmed with the natural woodwork and built-in storage cabinets typical of a Craftsman-era home. It was filled with personal things, too—flowering plants, copper cookware—and a small rectangular table with a banquette that probably wasn't original to the house. Still, it suited her.

"Oh, I do!" Holly said, smiling. "I'll show you." She disappeared around the corner to the living room and then returned a few minutes later, balancing an opened book in her arms.

"See?" she said, nodding down at the opened pages. She moved closer to him, their heads almost touching as they looked at the photographs she'd marked. "It'll look just like this when I'm done."

Her hair brushed his arm. Sam's skin prickled with goose bumps. God, he couldn't remember when he'd had a response like that to a woman. It felt good. It also felt like he was seventeen again, trying to hide a surprise erection behind his history textbook.

Grinning to himself, Sam concentrated instead on the

pictures Holly was showing him, squinting down at the series of interior and exterior shots of another Craftsman-style house. This one had been gussied-up like a museum, with period furniture and hardwood floors you could probably see yourself in.

"It's the most perfect example of the style I could find. What do you think?" Holly asked.

Sam thought it looked like a house that ought to be roped off so visitors could pass through without messing anything up. "Well," he equivocated, "this house is in Massachusetts. It would be hard to duplicate the effect out here in the West. What kind of modifications did you have in mind?"

"Modifications?" She looked puzzled. "Like what? This house is perfect."

Sam looked at the photos again, trying to place Holly inside them, inside that house. He couldn't do it. It looked too stiff. Unapproachable.

"It's too perfect. Maybe that's the problem," he said.

Holly shook her head. "That's ridiculous. It can't be too perfect."

"You've got to be able to live in the house, too. This house—" he tapped the photo with his fingers "—wouldn't work in Arizona. The landscaping is all wrong for the climate, for one thing. The chairs look about as comfortable as stadium bleachers, and these bare windows here look nice, but unless all your neighbors live five miles away, you're going to want some shutters or blinds for privacy. And—"

Holly snapped the book shut, all but flattening his nose with the pages in the process. Sam felt about as popular as the hunter who shot Bambi's mother.

"Okay," he said quickly, "you don't want me messing around with your design. Understandable. It's perfect. But maybe, just maybe, it's not right for this house."

Holly frowned, drumming her fingertips on the book.

"Renovating a house can be tricky," Sam said. "If you're not careful, it's easy to design the heart, the *you*, right out of it. Your house has a history. It's had generations of owners. Every one of them touched these walls"—Sam reached for her hand and pressed it, warm beneath his, against the white plaster wall—"and left something here. Now it's your turn."

Beneath his palm, Holly's hand trembled. He brushed his thumb along the edge of hers, downward to her wrist, easing the pressure of his grip in case Holly wanted to move away. She didn't. Sam moved closer, until they were only inches apart. She was still, watching him. She was warm, luring him. She was sexy as hell, surprising him. Sam took the only action that seemed reasonable under the circumstances, and kissed her.

His thoughts were veering into new and dangerous directions by the time Holly ended the kiss.

"Do you always win arguments this way?" she asked, managing to look both hot and bothered, and just plain bothered, as she clutched the book to her chest.

"Nah. Sometimes I need a rebuttal," he murmured, lowering his mouth to hers again. God, she felt good. Kissing Holly was like eating chocolate for breakfast—pleasurable, sweet, but probably not very smart.

She dropped the design book on his foot.

"Ow!"

"Ooops, sorry," she said, looking not the least bit repentant. She whipped her hand out from beneath his, then bent to pick up the book and thumped it onto the countertop. "Listen, Lothario," Holly said, "I think we need to get a few things straight."

"Can we wait until my foot quits throbbing? That damn book must weigh at least ten pounds."

She shook her head. "Number one, I didn't invite you over here so you could perform some pizza and wine seduction routine on me. That was a cheap shot—"

"A double deluxe pizza from Angelo's isn't all that cheap," Sam argued. "Have you got any aspirin?" he added, tugging at his boot. If the pain was any indication, he'd lay bets his big toe was broken.

Holly, clearly not a woman to be jollied out of her agenda, cast him a scathing look. "You'll be fine. It's not that heavy a book." She continued talking, ticking off items on her fingers as she went: "Number two, I wanted your opinion on my house renovation, but you just wrecked my whole vision. Have you ever heard of tact?"

"You asked what I thought. I was supposed to lie?"

Shaking her head, she paced into the living room. "How do you ever get any jobs, anyway?" Holly waved the question away. "No, never mind, don't answer that. I think I know."

Carrying his boot, Sam followed her. "What the hell does that mean?"

Holly faced him. "Oh, come on. I saw how you worked on the waitress this morning at the Downtown Grill, doing that . . . that *smile* thing you do, all oozing charm. I've got to say, it worked like a dream. I'll bet you get great service, don't you?"

"*Oozing charm?* Yuck." He shuddered. "I get jobs because I'm good at what I do. Period."

" 'Course, it doesn't hurt when your father's the biggest contractor in Saguaro Vista, does it? Half the town must work for him," she shot back.

Wham, direct hit. Sam scowled. "You don't know what the hell you're talking about. I do not get hired just because of who my father is. Besides, that's just my summer job," he told her. "The rest of the year I have a perfectly respectable job in Tucson, remember?"

"Whatever," she said infuriatingly. Then, undaunted, Holly waggled three fingers at him. "Number three, I happen to have a boyfriend that—"

"That you're separated from?"

"That I care about very much," she said staunchly, heading back into the kitchen. Sam followed, stopping beside the refrigerator to massage his injured toe.

Holly picked up a towel, polishing the porcelain sink and backsplash with far more attention than the already spotless surfaces deserved. She poured more wine, set the bottle down, then picked it up and poured a little more. Carrying the bottle and her glass, she paced back into the living room.

Sam followed, having visions of tying Holly to a chair so he could stop hobbling after her on his one good leg. "What's the matter? Having trouble thinking up a fourth objection?"

He regretted the words the minute he saw the wistful expression on her face. He'd rather have her drop ten books on his toe than look like that, Sam realized.

Holly looked forlorn. "I guess Clarissa told you about me and Brad?" she asked.

He nodded. "Unless there's more than one Brad the Bad?"

"Nope." She dropped into a big, flowery-upholstered chair and took a hefty swig of her wine. She sighed. "There's only one."

He settled onto the sofa, opposite her. "Why does Clarissa call him Brad the Bad, anyway?"

"You really can't guess?" Holly eyed him curiously. "Then I'm not volunteering. Let's just say Clarissa never liked Brad much, and leave it at that, shall we?"

"Sure." Sam wasn't in any hurry to repeat what Clarissa had told him, anyway—that Holly took in wrong men like other people took in stray dogs, and had about as much success domesticating them. Despite her crack about nepotism, he just wasn't feeling that mean. Besides, it wasn't any of his business.

"On a completely different subject," he said instead, "how much are you asking for rent? I'm assuming you're still in the market for a roommate, unless you found somebody since this morning?"

Holly choked on a mouthful of wine, bringing on an impressive coughing attack. Once her breathing had returned to normal, she asked, "You're still interested?"

Sam grinned. "I don't scare easily."

"Hmmm?"

"Nothing. How much?"

She told him the rent. "But don't feel put on the spot just because Clarissa asked you to meet me," she emphasized. "I know she must've put you up to this, but it's really not necessary."

Holly narrowed her eyes and gave him a speculative look. "Besides, I'm not so sure you're the right roommate for me. I can't go around dropping things on you every day, you know."

"I didn't make the offer because of my cousin," Sam assured her, gingerly propping his injured right foot onto the coffee table. "And I promise I'll behave. From now on, I'll ask first before I kiss you."

She scrunched up her nose at him. "And I'll say no every time, guaranteed," she promised.

He laughed. If her participation in their last kiss had been so reluctant, he couldn't wait to find out what Holly was like when she felt enthusiastic.

"You know," she continued, "Maybe I could do without a roommate altogether. It would probably only be for a few months, anyway, and I've got enough saved to cover that."

Holly finished her wine and set the glass on the table, then glanced around the living room. Her gaze settled on the fireplace, the centerpiece of a cozy inglenook formed by the built-in benches and a pair of tall bookshelves that flanked it on both sides. It was a typical Craftsman construction, spoiled only by the hunk of nailed-on plywood that sealed the fireplace shut.

"The money you've saved—it's your renovation money, isn't it?" Sam asked.

She looked at him, surprise evident in her expression. "How did you know?"

"A wild guess." He readjusted the angle of his foot on the coffee table, grimacing at the pain the movement brought him. He didn't want to be a baby, but his toe hurt like hell. It would be a bitch driving back home.

"If I move in for the next few months—say, until the end of August—it'll be good for both of us. You'll be able to put your renovation money to its intended use— restoring your house. And I'll already be here, so working on your renovation will be a snap. As a bonus, I won't have my mother hovering over me while I'm in town, trying to make me eat my vegetables like I was still six years old."

She smiled. "With my mom, it's milk. 'Does a body good!' I think I'll need to be completely gray-haired before she believes I'm a grown-up."

They laughed. Sam leaned forward. "Do we have a deal?"

Holly still looked hesitant. "What about my design plan? We didn't exactly agree on renovation ideas, you know."

"Tell you what," he replied, "all I ask is you let me make my case for an alternate design. If you don't like it, okay. We'll go with your idea instead. The decision's all yours to make."

"Very gracious of you ... considering the fact it's *my* house under discussion here," Holly said. Then she smiled. "Just kidding. That sounds like a workable compromise to me. When do you want to start?"

"Let's hammer out the details tomorrow over breakfast," Sam said. Holly nodded. Grinning, he added, "Shall we seal the deal properly?"

"What?"

"With a kiss," he explained. "Shall we seal the deal with a kiss?"

She stared at him for a second. Then, laughing, Holly put out her hand. "Are you a slow learner, or what?"

"Can't blame a guy for trying." Sam accepted the handshake she offered, then reached for his boot. "Now that that's done," he went on, "I need to ask you a favor."

"Umm, sure. What is it?"

"Would you drive me to the doctor? I think my toe is broken."

Chapter Three

"Oh, my God!" Holly bent over and peered at Sam's foot more closely. Now that he mentioned it, his toe *did* look a little ... unusual.

"Umm, you know the cartoon where the coyote has an anvil dropped on his foot and it blows up like a big furry balloon?" she asked, poking tentatively at his stockinged toe.

"Ouch! Yeah?"

"That was actually pretty good, compared to this."

"You're making jokes now?"

Holly glanced over at him. His eyebrows drew together, making him look surprisingly fierce. Clearly, he was not amused.

"You are. You're making jokes at an injured man's expense," Sam said. "I can't believe it."

Okay, so her jokes never did go over very well. That didn't mean she couldn't try to cheer him up, she reasoned.

"I'm sorry. I really am," she said, actually feeling fairly awful about smashing his foot with the design book. It had seemed like a good strategy at the time—she could hardly just let him maul her right in her own kitchen, could she? Great kisser or not, she barely knew him.

"Wait here," she told him, heading into the kitchen to get the phone. "I'll be right back."

"I'm a cripple, where am I going to go?" she heard Sam grumble as she passed him. Men acted like such babies when they were hurt. Holly felt bad about it, but it had been an accident, after all. She hadn't meant to *really* hurt him.

"I do *not* have furry coyote toes, either," he called from the living room. Holly hid a grin and dialed Brad's pager number. There were some advantages to having a boyfriend who was a doctor, even if they were temporarily separated. She was sure he'd agree to come over and have a look at Sam's toe injury. Brad liked to feel he was rescuing people; it was one of the things that made him a good doctor.

Not to mention the fact that a house call would save her and Sam a drive to the emergency room and probably a three-hour wait for a doctor there. And if Brad just *happened* to get a look at her hunky new roommate, well . . . what was wrong with that?

When Holly returned to the living room with a bottle of pain reliever, the rest of the wine, and Sam's wineglass, he eyed her warily.

"Here," Holly said, tapping some of the medicine into her palm and handing it to him, "this ought to help a little."

He squinted at the prescription label, then up at her. "How do I know you're not trying to poison me now?"

"Fine." She dropped the medicine back into the vial and snapped the lid on. It wasn't until Holly glanced up again that she realized Sam had been joking. He was smiling at her, giving her the same charm-oozing smile she'd accused him of using on the waitress. Suddenly the room felt too warm, their position too intimate, his appeal too dangerously real.

Too bad that smile worked so well on her, too.

The phone buzzed in her hand. Grateful for the opportunity to think about something else besides Sam, Holly answered it.

"Holly! I told you not to page me unless it was an emergency," Brad squawked into her ear. She'd forgotten how loudly he spoke on the phone, how overwhelming his presence could be, even long distance.

"It is an emergency," she said, covering the phone with her hand and mouthing "It's Brad" to Sam. He looked interested, if a little confused.

"The Bad Boy himself?" Sam asked. Holly frowned and waved her hand at him to be quiet.

"Can you come over here, please?" she asked Brad. "I think my new roommate has a broken toe, and I was hoping you'd take a look at it."

"I'm a G.P., not a podiatrist. Can't you just take her to the emergency room? It's getting late, and I've got appointments in the morning."

She couldn't believe he was arguing with her over this. "He's really in a lot of pain," Holly said, doing her best to ignore the way Sam was scowling at her and waving his hands. She might have known not to make the awful admission he was in pain, especially to another man.

The phone line was silent. "Brad? Just come on over, okay? For Pete's sake, I'm sure Sam will pay you, if that's what's worrying you."

She could practically hear his interest sharpen. "Sam?"

"My roommate. I told you someone was moving in, remember? Don't tell me you didn't believe me . . ."

He hadn't believed her. Holly could hear it in his voice as Brad went through some lame explanation about how rushed he'd been the last time they talked. She smiled, feeling less and less *un*spontaneous by the second.

"Elevate the foot," Brad said. "I'll be there shortly."

The line went dead. Holly blinked, then replaced the phone in its stand, and turned to Sam. "He's on his way."

"It's broken, all right." Brad pinched Sam's bare big toe between his fingertips and waggled it a little. Sam turned gray, but remained silent. Good thing, too—he appeared to be biting back several choice words, and Holly doubted whatever came out of his mouth would be polite.

"Try to stay off of it as much as you can," Brad said. "Call my office if the swelling doesn't go down or if it feels more uncomfortable, rather than less."

He straightened, pulling his car keys from his pants pocket and turning to leave. Holly grabbed his arm to stop him.

"Let you know if it gets uncomfortable? That's it?" she exclaimed. "You're just going to pack up and leave now? What about medicine, what about a cast?"

She looked from Sam to Brad and back again. She'd arranged poor Sam on the sofa as comfortably as she could, with his bare foot propped up on both pink-fringed throw pillows. It might have been a mistake to use two pillows— she'd somehow elevated his toe to roughly nose-height. Holly made a mental note to try a single bed pillow instead and turned to face down Brad.

Horribly enough, he looked about to laugh. "I can't put

a cast on a toe, Holly. A broken foot, sure, but not a broken big toe."

"Must be tough to maneuver around all those other toes, eh Doc?" Sam quipped from the sofa.

Holly didn't find Sam's pain funny in the least. "I want you to do something right now, Brad. There must be something you can do to help Sam."

Sighing, Brad took off his glasses, holding them in one hand while he rubbed the bridge of his nose.

"Brad!"

"I've done all I can." He handed one of his business cards to Sam, shaking his head sympathetically. "What did you do to him, anyway, Holly?"

"Me?"

Sam looked at her with renewed curiosity.

"Yes, you," said Brad. To Sam, he added, "Watch out, this woman's a walking recruiter for personal injury lawyers. One time she knocked a ladder out from under me when I was changing a light bulb, way up near this ridiculous high ceiling. I took the whole light fixture down with me."

They all glanced upward. "I just bumped into the ladder," Holly protested.

"Another time she threw a cast-iron skillet at me." Brad spread his thumb and forefinger a couple of inches apart. "Missed me by that much."

"I did not! The handle was hot, and I let go of it too quickly, that's all." As an aside to Sam, she explained, "I was concentrating on a new recipe. I told him to stay out of the kitchen." She glowered at Brad.

" 'Course, it's not limited to other people. Did Holly tell you about the time she bashed herself with a garlic press? Gave herself a really bad bruise on the collarbone," he went on blithely. "I wouldn't have thought kitchen utensils were so dangerous."

To his credit, at least Sam didn't laugh. Most people laughed at the garlic press story.

"Then there was the time—"

"That's enough for now, don't you think?" Holly interrupted, steering Brad toward the front door. "Thanks for stopping by. Let Thomas know I'll be calling him tomorrow to get a second opinion on Sam's toe, would you?"

Thomas White was Brad's partner, the doctor he shared office space with. Brad would've preferred his own office, Holly knew, but he couldn't afford to go it alone yet.

"Thomas is an obstetrician," Brad told her. "Toes are hardly his specialty. Take my word for it—all that's required is rest. Sam will be fine."

Sam waved from the sofa. "Thanks, Doc. And thanks for the warning, too," he added with a grin, nodding toward Holly.

She scowled. So much for making Brad jealous with her new roommate. Instead Brad and Sam seemed intent on doing some sort of male-bonding thing, although she couldn't imagine why. They had nothing in common, aside from gender: Brad was a successful doctor, respected by his peers. Sam was . . . not. Brad was organized, neat, ambitious, and blessed with model-good looks. Sam was . . . actually kind of scruffy-macho-looking, and if he were any more relaxed, he'd be asleep.

And now he was her roommate. Holly hoped she'd done the right thing. Closing the front door again, she glanced over at him.

"You and Brad don't go together very well," Sam remarked. The pain reliever she'd given him must have taken effect, because he seemed in much better spirits than he had earlier.

"What makes you say that?" Holly fluffed up the throw pillows in the brown armchair Brad had been sitting in, then bent to brush a piece of lint from the edge of the sofa.

"For one thing, you didn't give me your business card ten minutes after we met," Sam replied, dropping Brad's beige engraved card onto the coffee table.

Holly scooped it up and put it beside Sam's wineglass, where he'd be sure to remember it later. "I didn't do your bookkeeping, either," she pointed out in Brad's defense.

"If I had, you can be sure I'd have given you my card, too."

"Okay, then," he replied, "for another thing, you wouldn't have embarrassed a friend for the sake of a funny story."

"I wasn't embarrassed," Holly lied. So what if she was a little sensitive to Brad's teasing? It would've been much more embarrassing to admit her embarrassment. Besides, when she and Brad went to parties together, everyone else seemed to find his jokes funny.

"Anyway, how do you know I wouldn't?" she protested. "You don't know—maybe I go around lampooning my friends all the time."

"Mmmm," Sam grunted noncommittally. "I doubt it."

Holly raised her eyebrows.

"I can't explain it," he said with a shrug. "But I still think it's true—the two of you don't mesh."

Holly didn't know how true that could be when he couldn't even explain it properly. She shrugged right back at him. "You're wrong. Brad and I are perfectly well suited for one another."

"Well suited?" He made a face.

She'd definitely have to think up another phrase to describe her relationship with Brad.

"Yes," she said. "Brad is exactly the kind of man a girl dreams of. Even my mother loves him," she added. It was true. Her mom had all but hired the Goodyear blimp to broadcast the news when she'd begun dating Brad-the-doctor.

Sam looked up at her, and for once his expression was serious. "Do *you* love him?" he asked.

For all his seriousness, Holly hadn't expected *that*. "Of course—why wouldn't I? Brad and I had planned a nice life together."

What a strange thing for him to ask. She leaned closer to Sam, intent on picking up the wine bottle so it wouldn't leave a ring on the coffee table. The next thing she knew, he'd caught hold of her arm and was gently pulling her down.

"Sounds real cozy," Sam said. "Like a stockbroker's convention."

Holly had to brace one hand on the sofa back to keep from toppling into his lap. Their faces were only inches apart.

"And anyway, you can't plan love," Sam added quietly. "Brad doesn't deserve your loyalty."

"It's not just—"

Sam pressed a fingertip to her lips to quiet her. Holly was too surprised by the tenderness of the gesture to move away.

"I had to know," he said. "I had to ask, because even though we just met this morning, Holly—I'm already crazy about you. I had to know if there's a chance for us to—"

Crazy about her? How could that be? Stunned, she tried to pull away. His hand on her arm held her still for the rest of his words.

"—If there's a chance for us to be together. I know this sounds crazy. I always thought love at first sight was just another name for lust, but now . . . well, now I think maybe it's more than that."

"Sam—" Her voice failed her. Holly took in a huge breath and tried again. "I don't—"

"I do want you," he said quietly. "I'd be lying if I said I don't. But that's not all there is to this." His gaze shifted from her eyes to her face; he moved his hand higher, and she felt his thumb stroke across her cheek like a tiny caress. The way he looked at her was somehow curious, appreciative, and unmistakably honest, all at the same time. This couldn't be happening. Holly pushed away from the sofa, away from him.

"You've had too much wine," she said, grabbing for the wine bottle and nearly clobbering his injured foot with it in her rush to get away from him. "And maybe too much pain reliever, too. I'm sure you won't remember any of this in the morning."

Sam didn't move. "Yes, I will. I didn't have that much wine. And even if I didn't remember it, you would. You'd remember, and wonder, and pretty soon we'd be right back here talking about it again. We might as well deal with it right now, don't you think?"

Holly thought she might be hyperventilating. "This is insane," she managed to say. Then she made good her escape to the kitchen, leaving Sam stranded atop his pillows and hopefully unable to follow her.

She didn't know what to do. He'd seemed perfectly sane earlier. Holly set down the wine bottle, saw that her hand was shaking, and hugged both arms around herself to keep that shaky feeling from spreading to the rest of her. It didn't work.

Clarissa wouldn't have pushed so hard for this roommate arrangement if her cousin really was unbalanced, would she? No, of course not. Clarissa had known Sam since childhood; surely he couldn't have hidden some kind of crazed love-at-first-sight tendencies for that long.

Maybe this was just Clarissa's twisted idea of a practical joke, Holly thought. It was possible; she'd been the unwitting victim of a number of her best friend's schemes— usually they were funniest to Clarissa. Sidling up to the doorway, she peered around the corner at the back of Sam's head, fully expecting him to be convulsed with laughter that the joke had gone over so easily.

He wasn't laughing.

Okay, so that wasn't it. Turning, Holly finished the last dregs of red wine straight from the bottle and thought about it some more. Maybe Sam was one of those people who fell in love easily. Maybe he'd just broken up with another woman and he was on the rebound, wanting to salve his ego with the nearest skirtwearing remedy. Maybe this was simply another attempt to get her into bed, since the kiss hadn't worked earlier.

More likely, she was blowing the whole thing way out of proportion, Holly chided herself. Straightening her shoulders, she headed back into the living room and sat down in the chair across from Sam. She folded her hands in her lap, then looked over at him.

"I don't believe in love at first sight," she said.

"Me, neither," Sam replied. "At least, I didn't when I woke up this morning."

"It doesn't make any sense," she went on.

He nodded. "I know."

Holly flung both arms wide. "See? You're proving my point!" She'd finally met somebody who was even worse at arguing than she was. "It's impossible—we barely know each other. You can't love somebody you don't really know."

Sam grinned. He did that a lot, she noticed, unlike Brad. Brad had really missed his calling as one of those guards in London who were never allowed to smile.

There she went again, comparing the two of them. That had to stop. It wasn't fair to anyone.

"We should get to know each other better, then," Sam said.

For some reason, those words made her feel even more panicked than before. Determined not to show it, Holly said, "Well, we're going to be roommates. I guess we'll have plenty of time to get acquainted."

"I'm looking forward to it." He glanced pointedly at the empty spot beside him on the sofa. "Why don't we start right now?"

He should have looked ridiculous, a big, brawny man like Sam with his foot propped at nose-height on those pink-fringed pillows. He should have looked crazy, going on about love at first sight like he had. The trouble was, he didn't.

This spontaneity business wasn't all it was cracked up to be, Holly thought. Agreeing to let Sam move in for the summer was the most spontaneous act she could remember making, and already it was throwing her nice, steady life out of whack.

But Brad leaving her was what had really messed everything up. If seeing her with a roommate like Sam could bring Brad back to his senses—and there was still a good chance it could—it would be worth it. She and Brad made sense together. Holly had to do all she could to rebuild their relationship—to make her life the way it used to be.

Sam was still watching her, still waiting.

Holly sighed, but didn't move any closer to him. "I have to be honest, Sam. What I said before is true—I'm trying to work things out with Brad. Even though we're . . . apart . . . right now, I haven't given up on him yet. I can't."

He was silent, thinking. After a minute, he said, "I hope Brad knows how lucky he is. I wouldn't have let you go in the first place."

"Thanks."

It was sweet of him to say that. But Holly had no intentions of letting Brad let her go, either; her Plan was set to go into motion tomorrow.

"I think I'll be able to change Brad's mind," she said. Then she stood, turning toward Sam with both hands on her hips, and summoned up a businesslike tone. "As for you, you're not looking so good—"

"Thanks."

She grinned. "That's not what I mean. I think you should get some rest, though, and I've got an early day tomorrow. Are you going to be all right driving home?"

Sam flexed his injured foot, then glanced up at her. "If I said I wasn't, then what?"

Then I'd say, "Stay with me tonight." The thought came out of nowhere. Holly blinked. Obviously the events of the past week had affected her more than she'd thought. She was lonely without Brad, that was all—lonely and vulnerable and not at all looking forward to crawling into that big empty bed all alone again tonight.

"Then I'd drive you home myself," she said, forcing a certainty into her voice that she didn't really feel. "I could pick you up again in the morning, or . . . or whenever you decide to move in . . ."

"Is tomorrow too soon for you?" Sam's gaze caught hers and held, clear and blue and much too perceptive for her peace of mind.

"Not at all." If she was going to be spontaneous, Holly was going to do it all the way. "The sooner the better."

"Tomorrow it is, then." Leaning forward, Sam lifted his foot from the pillow pile and onto the floor, then held up a hand to her. "Can I trust you to help me up, or is that just asking for trouble?"

"Very funny." Holly caught hold of his hand. He squeezed back, and she looked down at their coupled hands. His was bigger, stronger, browner—so different from hers. It was . . . it was stupid to stand there staring at his hands. She dug her heels into the rug and pulled.

She realized her mistake in the same instant the rug slid across the glossy hardwood floor. By then it was too late to correct it. Holly fell forward on top of Sam, landing with enough momentum to roll them both hard against the sofa back.

She lifted her face from his shirtfront, shook her hair out of her eyes, and found herself plastered against him from chest to knees. She was all of four inches from Sam's face.

"I think you have an unconscious desire to be close to me," he said, unsuccessfully trying to hide a smile.

"You did that on purpose, didn't you?" she shot back.

She tried to wriggle backwards so she could stand up. It didn't work, partly because Sam's strong arm around her waist kept her there, and partly because she was afraid to wriggle too hard and accidentally hurt him again.

"I didn't do anything," he said. His chest rumbled against hers as he spoke. They were much too close. Holly wriggled a little more.

Sam's eyelids lowered slightly, and she would have sworn he was looking at her lips. Her stomach did a flip. She wriggled in earnest.

"Mmmm. That feels good."

She stopped cold. He was right; it did feel good—really good. She was still thinking about that fact when Sam's hands slipped from her waist and started moving toward her hips in long, slow arcs. Holly sucked in her breath, her attention temporarily caught by the feel of Sam's hands on her body. His fingers, warm and sure, traced a path over her lower back and downward.

Reality came crashing back.

"Another inch further south," she said, "and our roommate arrangement is history."

His hands lifted. "I thought you were enjoying it."

She was. Holly would've died before admitting it. She pushed up on her elbows and Sam let her go. After a bit of maneuvering, she wound up on her knees on the sofa, leaning in any direction but his. It wasn't a very dignified position, but she did her best to sound dignified anyway.

"I think you'd better go," she said.

Miraculously, he managed to get to his feet on his own power. She guessed keeping the renovation job and retaining their roommate arrangement was a powerful incentive. Either that, or Sam really couldn't stand another summer living with his vegetable-pushing family.

"Mad at me?" he asked.

Holly let her glare speak for itself.

"You're the one who jumped on top of me," Sam replied with an overly innocent lift of his eyebrows. He was obviously enjoying himself.

"I'll make sure it doesn't happen again," she told him as she stood, angrier more at herself than at him. Her knees felt wobbly. That unsteady sensation got even worse when Sam put both hands on her shoulders.

"There's something between us, Holly," he said, "and I know you can feel it, too. You can't ignore it forever."

Oh, yes, she could. She could ignore it, and she would. All she felt for Sam was the same garden-variety lust any woman would feel if she were plastered up against more than six feet of hard-muscled male. Nothing more. She wasn't going to wreck her future to satisfy it.

"I don't know what you're talking about," Holly lied, staring out the darkened window behind Sam so she wouldn't have to meet his eyes.

"Mmm-hmm." He squeezed her shoulders, then let his hands fall to his sides again. "Okay, if that's the way you want it."

She nodded. "It is."

It was. It was exactly the way she wanted it, Holly reminded herself as she handed Sam his boot at the door.

It was the only way it could be, she told herself as she watched him get into his truck and drive away. It was the smartest decision she could've made, she congratulated herself afterward, when she got into bed and turned out the light.

It was the loneliest night she'd ever spent, she thought to herself an hour later, when she still couldn't sleep. So she got up again, took out her day planner, and set about remedying the problem.

Chapter 4

That weekend, Holly drove with Clarissa to their favorite mall at the edge of Phoenix, a forty-five-minute drive from Saguaro Vista. It was the preparatory phase of her Plan—materials gathering.

"We must've been insane to come here on a Saturday," Clarissa said, waving her arm at the throng of mall-shoppers that streamed past them on both sides. "This is like feeding time at the zoo."

"I know," Holly said, clutching the shoulder strap of her purse tighter against her shoulder. They dodged two teenagers running past them, maneuvered around a pair of women pushing tandem strollers, then edged past a clump of men hypnotized by the big-screen showing of a basketball game at the electronics store.

"Have you ever noticed those stores never show anything but sports on those big-screen TV sets?" Holly asked, panting a little. Following Clarissa through the mall was a triathlon-worthy event.

"That's because purchasing power comes with a Y-chromosome, didn't you know?" Clarissa replied with evident sarcasm as they veered into the potpourried atmosphere of the lingerie store next door. "Besides, it makes the balls look bigger."

She grabbed something from the nearest rack and held it out for Holly's inspection. "Hey—what do you think of this?"

Holly shook her head. "That's not clothing. It's a shiny, hot pink hair elastic. That wouldn't cover more than ten percent of me."

"That's the idea." Clarissa threw back her head and batted her eyelashes, holding the lingerie on top of her T-shirt and jeans. "Brad'll love it," she promised.

"Absolutely not." Holly snatched the hanger. The pink spandex quivered as she shoved it back amidst its pseudo-satin companions. Why did those things need a hanger anyway? Any one of them could just as easily have been packaged in a number ten envelope.

"Brad has subtler tastes," she explained. "He's a classy guy. He doesn't like this kind of stuff."

Clarissa rolled her eyes. "All men like this kind of stuff," she said, sifting through a bin of thong panties. "How 'bout some of these? They're fifty percent off."

"There's a reason for that, I'm sure," Holly said, eyeing the panties skeptically. She picked up a white pair with pale pink flowers, the most subdued-looking in the bin.

"At least it's cotton." She looked at the price again. It really was a great deal, a third the price of her ordinary underwear. Maybe it would be a good compromise, plain in the front, but sexy in the back. She could just ease her way into the new, more seductive her—a woman Brad wouldn't dream of letting go.

Holly picked up a few more pairs in her size, holding them bundled against her chest while she went in search of Clarissa. She found her beside a display of garter belts.

"You need one of these, too," Clarissa advised, selecting a red satin one with black lace and waggling it toward her. She opened one of the drawers below the display and rummaged through it, presumably for a pair of matching stockings.

"Come on, this really isn't me," Holly protested, looking up at the bright rows of garter belts above Clarissa's head.

They looked like instruments of torture. "I don't even know how to wear one of these."

"It's very simple." Clarissa held up a pair of black seamed stockings, then glanced over at her thoughtfully. "What size, I wonder? How much do you weigh, anyway?"

"I'm going to tell *you?*" Holly shook her head vehemently and reached for the garter belt and stockings. "I'm sure these'll be fine."

She probably wouldn't be able to get up the nerve to wear any of it anyway. Hopefully she wouldn't have to, not if her other ideas to win back Brad were successful. Holly viewed a seduction attempt strictly as a last resort, but she wanted to be prepared for it, just in case. They moved on to the bras.

"Oooh—this one!" Grinning, holding the bra by its thin satin shoulder straps, Clarissa turned around. It was red, really red, look-at-me red. Appliquéd to the cups was a pair of what seemed to be black velvet hands, hands squeezing the . . .

"Oh, no. No." Holly shook her head.

"It's cute. You want to try it on?"

"No." Holly backed up.

Clarissa followed her with the bra. "Don't be a baby. It's about time you shed that Goody Two-Shoes image and started enjoying yourself a little."

Raising her eyebrows, Holly stopped. "Goody Two-Shoes?"

"You know what I mean." Clarissa pushed the bra forward. "Come on, it won't bite you."

Okay, maybe Holly was a little conservative, but she was no Goody Two-Shoes. Holly touched her fingertip to one of the appliquéd black hands. The velvet nap wiggled slightly beneath her finger. She squealed.

"This is too much."

"Trust me."

Clarissa pushed the bra into her arms. Holly couldn't give it back without dropping the garter belt, stockings, and thong panties she was already carrying. She squished it all into a tight, hopefully inconspicuous, lingerie wad, and followed Clarissa toward the rear of the store.

She was browsing in a corner nook labeled Couples Cove. The aroma of potpourri and scented candles was stronger here, and the lighting was dimmer.

"Just for inspiration, we'll get you a copy of the *Kama Sutra,*" Clarissa said, taking an ornate-looking book from the shelf. "And some of these"—she grabbed a fistful of brightly wrapped condoms—"and a couple of these."

She added two bottles, balancing them atop the book. Holly picked up one.

"Aphrodisia Massage Oil," she read aloud. She picked up the other bottle. "And Lover's Potion?"

"It's edible," Clarissa told her, looking helpful.

Holly dropped both bottles back into Clarissa's arms. "You've *got* to be kidding."

Clarissa's sigh was all the answer she needed.

"Have you and David actually used this stuff?" Holly whispered. She looked at her best friend with new eyes. Clarissa had always been more adventurous than she was, but this? And what in the world did that Lover's Potion taste like, anyway?

"The point is," Clarissa replied evasively, "that these things work."

Feeling doubtful, Holly raised her eyebrows.

"Okay, I can see I'm going to have to speak your language," Clarissa said. "It's been scientifically proven that these things work. Take the bra, for instance—"

As if on cue, one of the black velvet fingers popped out of the lingerie wad. Holly crammed it back in.

"Scientists have proven men respond best to red and black lingerie."

Holly made a face. Why couldn't men be attracted to a pretty floral print? Or, even better, why didn't they think a comfy pair of sweatpants and a T-shirt was the sexiest getup around? She said it aloud.

Clarissa ignored her. "Men also find the scent of vanilla

arousing," she explained, nodding toward the Aphrodisia Massage Oil.

She caught hold of Holly's sleeve and turned her toward the cash register. Just before they reached it, she added, "Oh, and one more thing. Be sure to leave the lights on."

"All the lights?" Holly said, aghast. Appear in front of Brad, illuminated by more than a hundred watts of cellulite-revealing lamplight? Or, God forbid, in daylight? He'd see every ripple, then demand she go running with him. The last thing she'd be feeling under those circumstances was sexy.

"At least one," Clarissa allowed. She put everything she'd selected onto the counter, then reached for Holly's lingerie wad and added that, too. Combined with the book, condoms, and exotic oils, it made for quite a risqué-looking pile.

"It's on me," Clarissa said as she handed her credit card to the clerk, a goggle-eyed teenaged boy. "Consider it a late Christmas present, if you want."

"I can't let you—"

Holding up her hand, Clarissa said, "I want to. Look, I know how much your Plan means to you. If this'll make you feel better, then I'm glad to help. What're friends for?"

Holly shook her head and handed over her credit card, snatching Clarissa's from the clerk's hand. He stared at them both. The shoppers in line behind them sighed.

"I'm paying." She said firmly. If she paid for it, then she wouldn't feel too bad about shoving the lingerie into a drawer until she found the necessary nerve to put it on. But if Clarissa paid for everything, Holly'd feel twice as obligated to wear it. Judging by the persistence with which her friend slapped another credit card down on the counter, Clarissa knew it, too.

"Humor me. You can pay at the next store. I might even let you pick out your own clothes," she promised with a grin.

The clerk scooped up Clarissa's credit card and scanned it before they could change their minds again. Case closed.

Five and a half hours later, they headed for the mall parking lot carrying enough sexy clothing to outfit the entire female cast of "Baywatch" on their off hours. Holly stopped beside her car, dropped her shopping bags onto the asphalt, and dug into her purse for her car keys.

"Mission accomplished!" Clarissa said, beaming. "I'll bet you thought it couldn't be done."

"Not for a second." Holly lifted the trunk lid. They loaded the shopping bags inside. Shopping exhausted her, but at least now she could consider part of her Plan completed. All she needed was an opportunity to put everything into action.

She slammed the trunk shut with a feeling of accomplishment. Now that she'd taken steps toward getting her life back to normal again, the future looked a little brighter.

Halfway through the drive to her house, Clarissa asked, "How'd it go with Sam last night? Did he like your house?"

The questions were put much too casually for typical Clarissa-speak. Holly glanced over at her, then back at the road.

"Fine," she said.

"Good. Sam's a nice guy."

"Except for his broken toe."

"What?"

Holly explained the book-dropping incident. She left out the kiss that prompted it, though. Somehow it felt too private to share.

"At least Brad the Bad was decent enough to pay a house call," Clarissa muttered, looking out the passenger-side car window. "I hope Sam'll be okay."

"I think he will be."

When Holly had phoned him earlier, Sam had told her he felt well enough to move in this afternoon. She'd promised to leave him a house key in one of the porch flowerpots. He might even be there when she got back home.

SURRENDER   57

Holly tried to imagine what it would be like to live with a man like Sam, a man so impulsive he'd give a woman a scorching kiss the day they met—a man who'd talk about love at first sight with someone he barely knew.

Holly turned down Clarissa's street. "Did you put Sam up to something last night?" she asked.

If she had, it would go a long way toward explaining Sam's behavior. Maybe the two of them had cooked up some sort of a joke after all and she'd fallen for it—hook, line, and sinker.

"Yes," Clarissa said. Holly's heart sank a little.

"It was my idea he meet you at the Grill. And I did encourage Sam to move into your place for the summer."

"That's it?"

"I wanted to help. God knows why you're so hung up on Brad, but I hate seeing you unhappy." *So there,* her expression seemed to say. "You promised Brad a roommate, and I helped deliver one."

Holly pulled into Clarissa's driveway. "Then you didn't . . . no, never mind," she said, turning toward Clarissa with a smile that felt patently false. "Thanks for wanting to help."

Clarissa wasn't having it. "Then I didn't . . . what?"

When Holly only drummed her fingers on the steering wheel and didn't answer, she pushed a little harder. "What do you think I did? Sam's a big boy, I can't make him do anything he doesn't want to."

Holly took a deep breath. "Last night Sam told me he was crazy about me. He said meeting me made him believe in love at first sight."

Clarissa's mouth dropped open. Good Lord—she'd rendered her speechless. Holly couldn't remember the last time that'd happened, if ever.

"This is still my cousin Sam we're talking about, right?" Clarissa asked.

Holly nodded. "Does he do this sort of thing a lot?" she asked, starting to feel concerned. Maybe Sam fell in and out of love with a different woman every week, maybe he was a closet Don Juan. For all she knew, he'd used this love-at-first-sight line before.

"As far as I know," Clarissa replied slowly, "Sam has never uttered the word love to a woman. Except maybe in bed," she amended thoughtfully, "but I wouldn't know about that, of course."

She pursed her lips and squinted at Holly. "Did you sleep with him already?"

"No!"

Clarissa looked at her closely. "Then why are you blushing, Holly-Berry? Hmmm?"

It was true; Holly felt the warmth spread through her cheeks and couldn't have stopped it to save her life.

"You've thought about it, then?" Clarissa pressed. "I wouldn't blame you, actually. Sam's quite a hunk—even I can recognize that, despite knowing him since he was a toddler."

A dreamy look came into her eyes. "We both used to get stuck at the kid's table together at Thanksgiving dinner, every year. We must've been twelve before we got promoted to the big table. And now Sam's falling for you. Wow."

"Clarissa—"

"It's okay, I won't breathe a word to your precious Bradley," she said, drawing out the name until it sounded at least six syllables long. A broad smile crept across her face.

"You and Sam," she muttered. "Wow."

"There's no me and Sam," Holly objected. "There's not going to *be* any me and Sam."

"I can't wait to tell David."

"Oh, no. You're not telling him a thing." If Clarissa's husband even suspected something was going on, the news would be all around town by bedtime. "Besides, there's nothing to tell. Nothing."

Clarissa picked up her purse and swung open the car door. She turned back to Holly, frowning in concentration.

"What's that saying?" she asked. "Oh, yeah—the lady doth protest too much, methinks." She winked and stepped out of the car. "I'll talk to you later," she called with a wave.

"Bye," replied Holly glumly. She was really in for it, now that Clarissa was on the case. Starting the car again, she pulled out of the driveway and headed for the only safe haven she knew—home.

Her safe haven had been destroyed.

Okay, maybe destroyed was a little harsh. Rearranged, redone—no, invaded—was more apt. In front, Sam's pickup truck was parked, two tires on the street, the other two on the sidewalk. Its bed was filled with assorted lengths of lumber, some bricks, and—Holly peered closer—a pair of old muddy shoes.

In the middle of the porch swing was a squat terra-cotta pot containing a miniature prickly pear cactus. Next to it was a longneck beer bottle. Just inside the doorway, she stepped over a green plaid flannel shirt. Beside the sofa lay a pair of very large tennis shoes. From the kitchen came the sound of an old Rolling Stones song, accompanied by loud male singing. Sam.

Holly sniffed. He must be cooking something, probably using her prized set of Calphalon cookware. The sauté pan alone cost more than a hundred dollars. She bolted for the kitchen.

What she smelled was dinner, but he wasn't cooking it, he was . . . agitating it. Sam held two white Chinese take-out cartons in each hand and he was swinging them by their wire handles to the beat of the song still blasting in the background. As she watched, he lifted his injured toe and spun on his heel, bopping across the kitchen floor, wiggling his backside as he went.

Holly smiled despite herself. Sam danced with the kind of abandon she hadn't witnessed since the drunken festivities at Clarissa's wedding reception.

"Hi," she called out. He shimmied across the linoleum, unable to hear her over the music and his own singing. Holly marched over to the portable stereo taking up most of the counter space in her little kitchen and switched it off. Sam paused in mid-spin, the take-out cartons still swinging.

"Great, you're home!" He didn't look the least bit chagrined to have been caught in mid-song. "Dinner's almost ready."

Holly slung her purse onto the counter. "You made dinner?"

"Don't go getting all mushy on me," Sam warned upon seeing her smile. "I just ordered in. It's nothing fancy."

From the looks of things, it was nothing neat, either. He hadn't left a stone unturned—or a cupboard door unopened. For the first time, Holly felt thankful for the meticulous order Brad had always insisted upon keeping everything in. Trying to look as unmushy as possible, she went through the kitchen flipping the cupboards closed.

Sam lifted the cardboard containers. "I was looking for some bowls to put these in," he explained. "Hungry?"

"Starving."

"Really?"

She nodded.

His smile grew wider and twice as seductive. "I've got just what you need," he teased. "Come on over and get it."

Did he really mean what she thought he meant? Sam leaned against the countertop watching her, his bare feet braced against the old linoleum floor. Holly let her eyes travel up the length of his denim-clad legs, past his haphazardly buttoned shirt, to his face. What she saw there made her tremble. He meant it all right, and every sensual spin she could put on the words. *Come on over and get it.*

Her breath left her. This was going to be harder than she'd thought.

"You probably want to bring in the things you bought first, though," Sam said. Holly's mind flashed on the supplies she'd purchased and the bags of lingerie, still in the trunk.

"You did go to the mall with Clarissa like you said, right? Do you want help carrying your things in?"

And let him see the stuff she'd bought? The red and

black velvet groping-hands bra? No way. She shook her head. "I . . . no, thanks. I can manage."

"Sure?"

Holly nodded.

"Okay, then," Sam replied, lifting the food cartons. "I'll get this ready while you do. Leave everything to me."

He couldn't know how tempting those words were . . . could he? Half on auto-pilot, Holly headed for the car to bring in the clothes she'd bought.

Just as she added the last shopping bag to the mountain of others on her bed, Sam called her for dinner. Walking back through the house, she felt his presence everywhere—saw it in the toothbrush beside hers that Holly glimpsed through the bathroom doorway, in the stack of unfamiliar books on the coffee table, in the baseball game that flickered on the television. It gave her a strange feeling. Until now a roommate had been just an idea, a faceless entity to make good her boast to Brad and help pay the mortgage. She hadn't counted on feeling Sam's presence so strongly.

Beneath the archway to the kitchen, Holly stopped and stared.

"Come on, it's getting cold," Sam said, when he glanced up and spotted her. The lights were dimmed, but just beyond him the banquette table glowed with light from the number of votive candles he'd set on it, along with the bowls of food. There were two place settings side-by-side on one long edge of the table, a teapot and cups, and a little pile of cellophane-wrapped fortune cookies for a centerpiece. Holly blinked. It was all still there.

"I thought we needed a better beginning than we had yesterday," Sam said when she reached the table. "Thanks for sharing your house with me."

"You're welcome," Holly heard herself say. She looked across the table again, wondering at a man who'd actually eat by candlelight without being cajoled into it. The food smelled wonderful, the table looked beautiful, it looked . . . it looked romantic. Holly raced for the light switch.

Sam's hand landed on top of hers before she could switch on the lights.

"Wait," he said, sliding his fingers beneath her palm and gently lifting her hand away. "Don't do that."

She glanced up at him. His fingers laced with hers and Sam came closer, closer until she was backed up against the wall behind her. His other hand came to rest on the wall beside her shoulder. He pressed forward, and Holly felt his hips touch hers, then withdraw. Her breasts grazed his shirtfront. When her nipples tightened beneath the layers of blouse and bra, her breath caught and held. What was he doing to her?

"I dare you," Sam said in a low voice. "I dare you to leave everything just the way it is. I dare you to leave it and see what happens."

He pressed their interlaced hands hard against the wall. "I dare you to feel, to feel us together. Feel me."

He was hard and hot and breathless, and she was melting against him. His hips rocked, once, sending the heat deeper through her, leaving her pulsing with sensation. *Feel, feel us together, feel me.*

"I can't," Holly gasped, ducking beneath Sam's arm. She took refuge on the other side of the banquette, the candlelight blurring from her sudden, inexplicable tears. Her whole body trembled with emotion. Whatever it was that Sam brought out in her, whatever he wanted from her, it scared Holly half to death. She couldn't look at him.

He switched on the lights, and Holly's breath returned with the brightness. Sam slid into the other banquette booth. For a long time, he didn't say anything—the only sounds were the clink of the teapot against the cups and the faint swirl of the tea as he filled each one. Steam rose up, fragrant and warm. Holly slipped her fingers around the heated cup and risked a glance at him.

"There's a sensuous woman inside you, Holly," he said quietly. "I think she's worth waiting for."

Holly shivered. No one had ever described her that way; she'd never thought of herself that way.

"Somebody ought to let her out," she joked, hoping to turn their conversation to safer ground. "It must be stifling in there."

Sam didn't smile. "You're the only one who can let her out."

He wasn't looking at her, and for that she was grateful. He picked up a plate and gestured toward the serving bowls with a spoon. "Want to try some?"

She could've cried with relief at his change of topic. Holly peered into the bowl. "What's in it?"

"I'm not sure. It's better not to look too closely at Chinese food." He grinned. "But it tastes great. You game?"

"Is there MSG in it? That's bad for you, you know. Some people have allergic reactions to MSG."

Sam paused, the spoon held a few inches above the bowl. "Do you?"

"I don't know. I don't want to find out, though."

"This allergic reaction—it's not fatal is it?"

"I don't think so, but—"

"Then the Kung Pao Chicken is worth it," Sam replied, scooping some onto the plate. He added a generous portion of beef with broccoli, then filled the remaining third of the plate with rice. He transferred a set of napkin-wrapped utensils from his side of the table to hers, then set the plate in front of her.

"Is this brown rice?" Holly asked, staring at it doubtfully. "Brown rice is healthier."

Sam shrugged. "I doubt it," he replied, ladling rice onto his own plate and topping it with heaping spoonfuls of both entrees. "Go on, try it."

It *did* smell good, she had to admit that much. Holly unfolded her napkin.

"It was nice of you to get dinner," she said, poking tentatively at an unfamiliar, very precisely-cut vegetable. Sam nodded, already chewing happily. Holly lifted a strand of something green and stringy between her fork tines and examined it. It looked like seaweed. She frowned.

"What's the matter?" Sam asked.

She twirled the seaweed around the fork and scooped

up some rice to help it go down easier. "I'm just not used to eating things I can't identify," she confessed.

"Then don't look," he suggested. "Just close your eyes and take a bite."

She was being a baby, Holly decided. Next thing she knew, he'd be suggesting she hold her nose, or take twenty-nine bites—one for each year of her life—like the lunch ladies used to do back in elementary school.

She ate the bite on her fork, then speared a piece of chicken and ate that, too. She was the new, spontaneous Holly, a lingerie-buying adventuress who lived to try new things.

"Like it?"

She was surprised to realize she did. "Mmm-hmm, it's pretty good."

It probably had a million calories, one plateful equivalent to twenty-five Big Macs or something, like that report on the movie theater popcorn. Heart attack on a plate. She ate some more. It was addictive, seasoned with flavors she didn't recognize and filled with weird vegetables, but Holly liked it.

Her eyes started to water. All of a sudden, her mouth was on fire. Her lips, her tongue—even her gums burned. Her nose started to run. She sniffed, swabbing at her watery eyes with her napkin.

"Sam," she choked out, hardly able to speak. "Sam!"

This was it. An MSG reaction. She was going to die from Chinese food. Holly waved her arm frantically.

He was beside her in an instant. "Here, drink this."

Holly gulped from the cup he held to her lips. When that was gone, she gasped and pointed to his cup, and drank all of his tea, too. By the time she'd finished the third cup Sam poured for her, she was starting to believe she wasn't going to die after all.

"My mouth is numb," Holly said, setting the cup back into the saucer and giving Sam an accusing glare. He retreated to his side of the banquette.

"Sorry. It didn't even occur to me you might never have

tried Chinese food. I guess it is a little spicy, if you're not used to it."

"A little spicy? That stuff could be used to keep peace between nations." She picked up her plate and pantomimed hurling it at an invisible enemy. "Watch out, or it's the Kung Pao Chicken for you!"

Laughing, Sam refilled both their teacups. Holly pushed her plate away. Far away.

"Maybe you ought to tell me what other things you haven't tried," he said, "so we can avoid disaster in the future."

He looked at her thoughtfully. "How about Indian food? Ever tried curry?"

She shook her head. "All these new things you've got planned for me to try—are they all food-related?" she asked, curious to know what else he'd suggest.

Sam smiled. Wickedly. "Not all of them," he said. "Ever try skinny-dipping? The weather's warm enough."

There's a sensuous woman inside you, Holly.

It was dizzying to keep up with him. One minute she and Sam were laughing, the next he was looking at her as if he wanted to devour her. No man had ever looked at her that way, not even Brad—especially not Brad. He was too self-disciplined for that.

" 'Course, I'd never ask you to do something you didn't want to do," Sam was saying.

Holly smiled. "I get the feeling we're not just talking about Kung Pao Chicken anymore," she said.

"I'm not. Where this takes us is up to you, Holly. But I think I can convince you to give us a try."

Sam unwrapped a fortune cookie and handed it to her, then selected one for himself. "You know, some people believe fortunes like these are really suppressed wishes," he said, cracking his fortune cookie open. "What do you think?"

"I think whoever's paid to write these things at the fortune cookie factory would be surprised to hear that," Holly replied, sliding the thin paper fortune out of her cookie.

"What does it say?"

"Your happiness is intertwined with your outlook on life," Holly read aloud.

"What do you think?"

"I think that could apply to about a million other people," she said pragmatically. "Yours is probably just as vague."

Sam shook his head. "I don't think so. I think it's right on target," he said, holding up the fortune so Holly could read it. She leaned forward.

"Your present plans are going to succeed," she read. Suddenly, inexplicably, her heartbeat quickened. With a deep breath, Holly glanced up from the paper fortune. Sam's eyes met hers and held.

"So," Holly asked, trying to sound lighthearted, "what are these big plans of yours?"

"To make you fall in love with me," Sam answered. He brushed his fingertip across the tip of her nose, then smiled. "I think it's happening already."

Chapter Five

Sam couldn't keep his romantic Chinese food dinner with Holly out of his mind. More than ever before, he felt the attraction between them growing. He made it almost four whole days before deciding to finish work early and finish what he'd started with Holly.

Of course, Sam's days always ended early whenever he was working on construction projects for his Dad's company—the crews started before sunrise to beat the early-summer Arizona heat. Going home at nine in the morning was equivalent to working a half day. He'd never taken advantage of being the owner's son before, but now that was exactly what Sam had in mind.

It was almost ten-thirty, on a day warm enough to heat

the black asphalt shingles that topped the house he and his crew were re-roofing. Even through his heavy-soled boots Sam could feel the heat radiating from the sunlight on the rooftop. Roofing jobs were a bitch in the summertime. With a longing glance at the swimming pool glittering in the house's yard below, Sam swiped his sweaty forehead with his forearm and turned his attention to his four-man crew.

"There's fifty bucks in it for each of you," he said, taking out his wallet, just to ensure their attention, "if we can get this job finished and cleaned up by eleven o'clock."

There was nothing like cold cash to motivate a person.

Before the hour was up, Sam was home in the shower. A half hour later, he drove up to the business complex where Holly's office was. His hair hadn't even dried all the way before he walked up to the receptionist's desk.

Her head was bowed while she penned a note in her spiral-bound message pad.

"Can I help you?" she asked, tearing the message from its perforated pad. She glanced up to put it in one of the boxes atop her desk, and saw him. She smiled widely.

Sam smiled back. "I hope so. I'm looking for Holly Aldridge. Is she back there?" he asked, nodding toward the rows of precisely arranged cubicles behind the receptionist's desk.

Her smile faded. So did much of her friendly attitude when she answered. "Ms. Aldridge is away from the office for the day. Perhaps another of our associates can help you?"

It was a rote reply. Sam tried again. "Can you tell me where she's gone?"

Holly hadn't been home, or he'd have seen her after his shower. And she hadn't mentioned anything about taking the day off, either. He wouldn't have thought anything short of a national disaster could pull Holly away from her desk. Even then, she'd probably grab a briefcase of work to take with her.

The receptionist frowned. "I'm afraid I can't tell you

Ms. Aldridge's plans, sir. Would you like to speak with someone else?"

Sir? Brrr, it was getting chilly in there.

"Sam, is that you?" Clarissa's head popped up over one of the fabric-covered cubicle partitions. When she saw it was him, she came around the corner.

"I'll handle this one," she told the receptionist.

After a quick hello hug, she took Sam's arm and herded him back toward her desk. Pushing aside some papers, her coffee cup, and a stack of computer CD-ROM jewel-cases, Clarissa settled one hip on her desktop.

"I thought I was hearing things," she said with a grin. "Turns out it really *was* you. You curious to know how the other half lives, or what?"

"What other half?"

"The responsible half. The grown-up half. The happily married and settled-down half."

"Oh, that half." Sam crossed his arms over his chest and leaned back, mimicking his cousin's relaxed posture. He added to it an affronted look. "I'm plenty responsible and grown-up," he informed her. "I've got a good job—"

"Which you treat like a lark," Clarissa interrupted with a toss of her hair.

"What?"

"Look at that ethics charge that old sour-butt Malcolm Jeffries brought up against you over changing your student's grade, for instance . . ."

Sam gave her a sharp look. Clarissa promptly waved it away. "Your folks told me. They worry about you," she said, answering his unspoken question.

Driving her point home with a jab at his midsection, Clarissa persisted. "Did you take care of that little problem yet? Huh?"

Sam felt a headache coming on. "The hearing's not for another month and a half," he said, "and it'll never fly. It'll blow over like all Malcolm's stupid charges have."

"You're probably right. Still . . ."

"Still, all that's beside the point," Sam went on, unwilling to devote any more thought to Malcolm Jeffries' petty machinations than he had to. Moving back to their original conversation, he said, "I have a good job, which is more than can be said for most of the yucks in this town."

"You have a job that allows you to feel like a student for the rest of your life. Admit it, Sam."

He didn't want to be drawn into that old argument again. Sam was the last person anybody in his family had expected to become a college professor. He knew that. Hell, he was the last person *anybody* had expected to go to college, period. The people close to him didn't understand his reasons for it, and Sam wasn't holding his breath until they did.

"Don't you have work to do?" he asked Clarissa.

She grinned. "It's more fun to badger you."

"I was afraid of that." Sam sighed and decided to get it over with. Clarissa wouldn't let up until she found out what she wanted to know.

"As for the rest of your accusations,"—he shot her a knowing grin—"I'll get married and settled down just as soon as Holly comes to her senses and says yes. Anything else?"

Clarissa shrieked. Several heads popped up over the cubicle partitions. Red-faced, she waved them back down again. She leaned forward and grabbed Sam's shoulder.

"It's true then! Oh, Sam—that's so romantic! Love at first sight. I'm really happy for you."

She sighed. "I can hardly believe it, but I'm really happy for you."

"Believe it. If you keep grinning like that, though, your boss is going to wonder what you're up to in here," he told her, unable to hang onto the disgruntled expression he wanted on his face.

Truth was, Sam felt like shouting from the rooftops how he felt about Holly. To him, she was the perfect combination—a woman who inspired love, respect, and mind-bending lust in approximately equal amounts. He grinned. The only thing stopping him from taking out a billboard to propose to Holly was the fact that she'd probably laugh in his face. He wasn't Dr. Brad the Bad, after all.

"Ohmigod!" Clarissa exclaimed, looking at him closely. "You really do mean it, don't you?"

Sam meant it like he meant to go on breathing, like he meant to wake up tomorrow morning. Like he meant to make Holly feel exactly the same way.

"When have you known me to be hesitant about something?" he asked, and Clarissa's eyes widened.

"Point taken." She hopped down from her desktop. "In that case, you'd better hurry."

"Why?"

"Because Holly's with Brad right now," she said, scanning the yellow sticky notes stuck all over her computer monitor. Selecting one, Clarissa explained. "That's the reason she took a personal day today. She's at the golf course, trying to talk him into giving it another go. It's part of her Plan."

"Her plan?"

"Holly would kill me if I told you any more. Just trust me, okay?" Peering at the sticky note, she dialed her phone and thrust the receiver into Sam's hand.

"She left me the golf course's number in case some work-related emergency came up," Clarissa explained, rolling her eyes. "Brad's tee-off time is noon. If you hurry, you can still catch up with them."

"And I want to do that because . . . ?"

Clarissa gave him a self-satisfied little smile. "Because you and Holly belong together, that's why. Why do you think I pestered you into moving in with her for the summer? Sheesh!"

"You set us up?"

His cousin the matchmaker nodded. Smugly.

"You've got to stop her, Sam. If I know Holly, she just might be able to wrangle Brad the Bad into a new commitment. One turn around the fairway—alone—might be all it takes."

Sam hung up the phone. He'd make all the neccessary arrangements with the golf course when he got there, he decided; after all, there was only one course in all of Saguaro Vista. Right now there was no time to waste.

Her new golf clubs hadn't seemed half so heavy inside the sporting goods store at the mall, Holly thought, struggling to get through the clubhouse door at the Saguaro Vista golf course without dumping the whole set onto the terrace. Slung over her back by the golf bag strap, they were awkward to carry; held in front of her, they blocked her vision. She tried tucking the bag partway beneath her elbow like a gigantic clutch purse, and nearly poked her eye out with a putter. Maybe hiring a caddie to help her would've been a good idea after all.

Then she saw Brad, standing just a few feet away. He gazed out across the fairway as though searching for someone, one hand shading his eyes against, Holly supposed, the blinding glare of the green. Despite the hundred and twenty dollars he'd paid for them, apparently Brad's designer sunglasses were no match for the immaculately kept, unnaturally green grass surrounding them.

Holly tried not to feel vindicated by that, but it was hard. She'd lobbied to spend that hundred and twenty dollars of joint-checking account money on something worthwhile, like a new pair of shoes. Brad had vetoed that idea in favor of the fancy sunglasses, although to his credit, he'd bought Holly a pair, too. Never mind the fact that she'd never held onto a pair of sunglasses longer than three months without laying them down someplace and forgetting them. Sometimes Brad just didn't make sense.

Today Holly was banking on Brad making sense. She needed him to listen to reason—it was the first phase of her Plan. They still hadn't discussed the reasons behind their separation, and Holly was through waiting for Brad to initiate that conversation. She wanted to get to the bottom of whatever the problem was, and solve it.

Holly felt sure that whatever Brad came up with, she could find a way to work around it. Just to be doubly sure, she'd even prepared a list of possible rebuttals. It was tucked inside her golf bag for quick reference, in case she got flustered and forgot one of the points she wanted to make. Holly felt you could never be too prepared.

Brad lowered his hand and headed toward the first hole. With a mighty effort Holly hefted her clubs again and hurried after him.

She set one espadrille-clad foot onto the fairway just as Brad disappeared behind a hill. Keeping her gaze fastened on the spot she'd last seen him, Holly quickened her pace. It wasn't easy to hurry wearing a sundress and cute new sandals and carrying a big leathery-smelling golf bag, but Holly was encouraged by the thought that she looked nice. She caught up to Brad only a few minutes later.

She plunked her golf bag down beside his. "Hi!"

Being apart from her hadn't affected his sense of style any, not if his neatly pressed khaki shorts and yellow polo shirt were anything to go by. Unlike some men, Brad took pride in dressing well and looking good, from his expensive haircut down to his discreetly manicured fingernails. He looked as great as ever, maybe even a little *too* polished. Suddenly, one of the qualities that had first attracted her to Brad seemed ... well, a little shallow.

Holly pushed away that disloyal thought. Where had that come from? She'd probably been influenced by living with Sam. She'd lay bets he'd spent more time arranging that Chinese food dinner for her than getting himself ready for it. The man just didn't care about nice clothes. It was rubbing off on her, now, too.

"Hi," Holly said again, smiling encouragingly.

Brad was surprised as all get out to see her there. She could tell by the way he leaned forward, raising his sunglasses a little to get a better look.

"Holly, what in the world are *you* doing here?"

"Thomas asked me to fill in for him," she replied. "An, errr ... emergency came up at the office."

Holly was the emergency. She'd cornered Brad's partner Thomas early that morning to ask him if he'd let her take his place in his regular Wednesday golf game with Brad. Asking nicely, cajoling, and pleading had no affect on him, but Holly'd finally gotten him to agree by promising to sell Thomas her fancy new golf clubs if things didn't turn out her way. Since she felt fairly confident Brad would respond to a reasonable conversation, it was a bet she'd been willing to make.

Brad frowned. "But you hate golf. You always refused to go with me." He shot a suspicious glance at her golf clubs. "You told me the grass they use on the fairway makes you sneeze."

"Guilty. I know I said all those things. But Brad,"—Holly moved closer to him, watching his gaze dip automatically to the heart-shaped neckline of her sundress—"I'm turning over a new leaf. When you left, I realized I was partly to blame, too. I spent so much time working, I guess I neglected you."

A measure of suspicion returned to his expression. She couldn't blame him. That speech was a little hard to swallow for her, too. Holly figured it was necessary to concede something—sort of a good faith gesture to open their negotiations.

"I want to share your interests, Brad. Like golf. So, here I am," she concluded with a nod toward her new golf bag.

"Whose is that, anyway?" he asked. It was a fine bag, the priciest in the store. It had come highly recommended from the salesperson. She'd wanted to impress her sincerity upon Brad, so she'd bought it. It looked like it had worked. He was all but drooling on the expensive leather.

"It's mine," Holly said proudly. "I bought it last weekend."

"Just in case a golf emergency arose?"

Whoops, he had her there. She blustered through it. "Yes. And since you're here, and I'm here, and Thomas isn't here, we might as well get started. You'll miss your tee time."

Helpfully, Holly dug into the side pocket of her golf bag and retrieved a handful of tees. She handed one to Brad.

"Ouch! You don't have to stab me with it." He glared at her, rubbing the palm of his hand.

"Sorry."

The first two holes went pretty quickly. Holly's shots were a little wide, but she thought she was doing well for a beginner. Brad wasn't quite as encouraging, but by the time they reached the third hole, he'd stopped telling her she was throwing off his entire game. She took that as a hopeful sign.

"Sure is nice and peaceful out here," Holly said as Brad lined up his next swing. "I don't even see anybody else playing nearby, do you?"

He grunted.

She went on: "I was just thinking, this would be a perfect place for a private conversation. Take us, for instance—we have lots to talk about."

He groaned. "You set me up, didn't you?"

Trying to look innocent, Holly took her time selecting a driver from her golf bag. "What's wrong with wanting to talk to you? I deserve an explanation for your leaving, Brad—something besides how you 'need your space.'"

She pulled out a club. A wood, Holly thought, or maybe it was an iron. She could never remember all the different names. She tried a practice swing with it, to give Brad time to respond.

"I knew it. This *is* a trap," he said. He gave her a dark look, hefted his bag over his shoulder, and set out after his ball. Holly stopped practicing her swing and took up the stance the guy at the pro shop had showed her. Aiming carefully, she whacked the ball before Brad could leave her behind.

It was a beautiful shot. It sailed cleanly into the air, higher than any shot she'd made so far, straight toward the next hole. Unfortunately, Brad's body was directly in the line of fire.

"Brad, look out!"

Holly was too far away to actually see the ball hit him, but she could tell when it happened, because he staggered backwards a bit. Clutching his shoulder, Brad bent down for the ball. She could practically feel the force of his glare as he stared up the fairway towards her.

Amazingly, though, when Holly finally reached him,

Brad was smiling. As she dropped her golf bag onto the grass and leaned on her club to rest up for the next shot, Brad tapped his pencil atop the scorecard in a cheerful manner that was exactly the opposite of what Holly expected.

"That's a penalty stroke for you," he said. "You're twelve over par."

Apparently a bruised shoulder was okay, as long as it helped him win the game. She hadn't realized Brad was so competitive.

"I'm sorry, that one just got away from me," Holly apologized, pantomiming the shot with her driver.

Brad glanced at her, then looked again. "No wonder that shot went wild, Holly. You're using a nine-iron."

She raised the driver and looked at its thick, sharply angled head. "I know. I like this one—it's got a little heft to it."

It seemed logical that a bigger club might give her a little bit of an advantage, since her opponent was bigger, stronger, and more experienced at the game. A look at Brad's face told her she'd reasoned wrong. Holly shrugged.

"You'll just have to teach me how to play, then," she told him, taking her errant ball from his hand and putting it back into play. "Next time, I'll be better."

Brad shook his head. "There's not going to be a next time. Golfing with you isn't an experience I want to repeat," he said. "You can't use a tee here," he added, watching her scoop up the tee she'd been about to plant on the green.

"I forgot," she muttered, tightening her grip on her golf club instead. "We need some shared interests, Brad," Holly went on, returning to the subject at hand. "How are we supposed to have a relationship, if we never spend any time together? A good relationship doesn't just happen. Both people have to work at it."

His lips tightened. "You know I hate talking about this relationship stuff," he said. He was looking straight at her, but Holly couldn't gauge a thing from his expression because of those stupid sunglasses. She stared back at him, expectantly. He sighed.

"I don't want a relationship that needs working at. If it needs so damn much work, maybe it's just wrong."

This wasn't what she'd expected. "That's not true—"

Brad gave a mean little laugh. "Oh, yeah—I forgot. I'm talking to the expert, aren't I?" The sarcasm in his tone hurt. "Far be it for me to second-guess Holly Aldridge, the relationship expert."

"That's not fair, and you know it," Holly managed to say, hardly able to believe what she was hearing. Didn't he care about salvaging things between them? If that was the case, even the neat, thorough list she'd prepared would be no help.

Brad put his arms around her shoulders. He shook his head. "I'm sorry," he said quietly. "But you keep pushing me to it. I told you this isn't a good time for me right now. I'm still adjusting to having my space."

He kneaded the tense muscles in her shoulders a bit, then dropped his hands. Brad peered into her face. "Better now?"

Holly nodded.

"Good. Let's get on with the game, then."

He rubbed his hands together and devoted his attention to choosing a driver for his next shot. Beside him, Holly did her best to regroup. She should've anticipated Brad's reluctance to discuss their relationship, but she hadn't.

She waited until they'd reached the back nine—and Brad was ahead of her by twenty-four strokes—before trying again.

"I thought things were going really well between us," Holly ventured as they walked together toward the tenth hole. As proof, she offered, "In the whole year we lived together, we never had a single disagreement. And we had such a nice routine going, just like an old married couple."

She smiled, liking the sound of that. It would be a good future, growing old together with somebody you loved. On the night of the romantic dinner that wasn't, Holly had been sure Brad was about to propose to her. The time had come. The dinner was meant as an encouraging push, just to let him know she was ready for a bigger commitment, too.

"Yeah," Brad muttered. "Just like an old married couple."

"You don't sound happy about that," Holly said, raising her eyebrows. "I thought—"

He stopped her with an irritated look. "Let's talk about this some other time. I can't concentrate with you yammering at me."

Holly took a step backward. Okay, a logical appeal wasn't working. She'd have to move on to the next phase of her Plan—an emotional appeal. Maybe Brad would respond better to a nonconversational approach. And if that failed, there was always the third and final phase of her Plan—seduction, although Holly didn't think she'd have to resort to such drastic measures.

Beside her, Brad frowned at the flag fluttering over the next hole, then peered down at his ball. Straightening his legs, Brad took his next shot. He was doing an excellent job of pretending she wasn't there. Holly might as well be invisible for all the attention Brad was paying to her. It didn't help her feminine ego any to recognize that fact.

In the distance, the buzzing sound of an engine drifted over the grassy hills between them and the clubhouse. It sounded like somebody mowing the grass, although that couldn't be, not while there were players on the course. Curious, Holly shaded her eyes with her hand and looked for the source of the sound.

A couple minutes later she saw it—an aqua-colored golf cart, coming straight down the path toward them. A lone man hunched a little over the steering wheel, driving at a speed that made the cart waver from side to side along the path. The vibrant-colored canopied top shimmied and snapped in the breeze as the cart came closer.

Brad looked up at it. "I didn't know those things could go that fast," he remarked, frowning. "Must be some hot-rod kid—"

His words faded when the cart squealed to a stop a few feet away from them. The driver got out and smiled.

"Sam! What are you doing here?"

It was wonderful to see a friendly face looking back at her. Feeling ridiculously glad for the interruption in her game, Holly waved for him to come nearer. He did, striding across the green with more casual ease than should've been possible for a man Sam's size—especially one with an injured toe. Brad, only as tall as Holly, was dwarfed beside him.

Sam shook his hand. "Hi, Doc. How's the game?"

"Fine, thanks." Brad surreptitiously slid the scorecard into his shorts pocket with his free hand. "Holly's having a little trouble, though."

Sam turned to her. "Oh, I don't know about that. I saw that drive you made back there. You looked good," he said.

The appreciative way his gaze roved over her new sundress made Holly wonder if it was really her golf form he was talking about. At the moment, though, she didn't care. She felt like soaking up the praise like a flower basking in sunshine.

"Thanks." She couldn't resist an I-told-you-so look at Brad before turning back to Sam. "Hey—would you like to join us? There's always room for one more . . ."

Brad snickered and elbowed Sam in the ribs, man-to-man style. "She's still got a lot to learn about the game," he said. Turning to Holly, he explained, "You can't add players midway through the course. Your friend here—"

"Sam," the friend in question supplied helpfully.

"That's right, I remember. Your friend Sam, here, will just have to wait for another time to play with you, Holly."

Sam waggled his eyebrows at her, turning Brad's comment into the most ribald of double entendres. "Okay," he said, grinning. "Guess I'll play with you later, Holly."

They both laughed. It was hard to remain serious with Sam around, Holly was discovering.

Brad wasn't laughing—he was staring impatiently at the

next hole. He cleared his throat. "Well, Sam, we've got a game to finish here, so if there's nothing else . . ."

"Actually," Sam said, "there is. I came out to get you, Holly. There's an emergency situation you've got to take care of."

Holly sighed. She might've known the instant she actually took a personal day—her first all year—a crisis would come up. She turned to pick up her golf bag, but Sam had already thrown it over his back and was carrying it to the cart.

"I'm sorry, Brad," she told him. He shrugged. He'd experienced enough work-related emergencies himself to know that she had no choice but to leave. It was a familiar pattern between them—even when they were living together, they'd seldom had the same days free from work.

"Let's get together in a few days. Is Francie's okay with you?" Holly asked.

She crossed her fingers, waiting for his answer. Brad couldn't refuse dinner with her at the restaurant where they'd had their first date, could he? It was the linchpin of the second phase of her Plan.

Brad didn't disappoint, at least in this instance. "Call my office. We'll arrange a time."

"Okay." With one last backward glance and a sigh for the failed first phase of her Plan, Holly headed for the golf cart where Sam waited for her.

Sam drove back to the clubhouse at a reasonable speed, now that he'd found Holly and gotten her safely ensconced on the golf cart seat beside him. As they reached the edge of the fairway, he glanced over at her.

"You look great," he said, looking over her short, flowery dress again. It ended a few inches above her knees and was held up by a couple of thin straps at the shoulders, the kind of thing that made him think of hot summer days at the beach. He liked it. He liked the looks of Holly wearing it.

It was a funny choice to wear golfing, though. He'd bet

Holly had meant to improve more than her golf scores with it.

"New dress?"

"Mmm-hmm," Holly murmured absently, digging around in her golf bag. She pulled out her fat day planner and rifled through it. "When my office called, did they tell you what the emergency is?"

He stopped the cart at the clubhouse. "Well," he said cryptically, "I didn't actually say it was an emergency at your office, now did I?"

Sam felt her suspicious stare on his back while he returned the golf cart keys to the attendant.

"What do you mean?" she asked when they were alone again, walking across the parking lot toward his truck.

"Don't get mad."

Holly stopped and stuck both hands on her hips.

"You look mad."

"You look like you've got some explaining to do," she replied, tapping her foot on the pavement.

"Okay." Sam slung her golf bag into the bed of his pickup, raising a cloud of dust as he did, and pulled out his keys. "Clarissa told me where you were when I ran into her at your office earlier today."

Holly's foot tapped faster. "What were you doing at my office?"

Why was she looking at him like that? "I was going to take you out to lunch," he replied, "but you weren't there. So I took a chance you'd say yes, and came out here to get you."

"Why do I get the feeling I've just been bamboozled out of my golf game?"

"Maybe because you were." Sam smiled, went around to the passenger-side truck door, and opened it for her. "Come on," he said. "I'll take you any place you want to go."

Holly crossed her arms over her chest. "I've got my car. I can drive myself."

"All right."

She didn't move.

SURRENDER

Stepping back to make way for her to get into the truck, Sam raised his eyebrows. "Would you rather go back to your golf game instead?"

She glanced back toward the fairway. "No . . . it wasn't exactly going the way I'd planned," she said cryptically.

Did that have something to do with the plan Clarissa had mentioned? Sam made a mental note to get more information about it from his cousin—the matchmaker.

Holly looked indecisive, as though torn between going with him and bolting for the security of her car. "Will you bring me back for my car later?"

Sam nodded, waiting.

Grumbling something about masculine ego, Holly uncrossed her arms and came to meet him beside the open passenger-side door.

"Does this mean you're not mad at me?" he asked, looking down at her.

"It means the pavement was burning my feet," she grumbled, waggling one sandal-clad foot in demonstration.

Sam grinned and gave her a hand up into the truck cab. She hovered above the bench seat, swiping away the dust, papers, and cassette tapes so she could sit down. Her voice, complaining about the messy state of his truck, came through the open window as he got in the other side.

"So what's the big emergency?" she asked once he was settled.

"Persistent, aren't you?"

She just looked at him.

"There's no emergency," he confessed, pulling the truck slowly into traffic. Sam shot a glance at her. "I just wanted to spend some time with you. How else am I going to convince you this love-at-first-sight thing is real?"

Her eyes widened.

"Put your seat belt on," he added.

He felt her eyes on him the whole time she was pulling the belt across her body and buckling it. Everything in her body language screamed wariness. Sam felt like smacking himself on the forehead. Idiot. Holly probably thought he was a love-crazed lunatic. He couldn't exactly blame her for it, either. He felt like one.

"You know, you can't just go around kidnapping people from golf courses," Holly said. "Does this ploy actually work for you?"

"Not all the time." Sam wasn't sure, having never tried it before.

Holly made a little harrumph sound. "I'll just bet. Where are we going?"

She gripped her day planner tight in both hands, probably ready to whack him with it if he got out of line. It looked heavy enough to give him a real shiner if her aim was good. Clearly Holly was a woman unused to spontaneous fun.

"We can go right back to the golf course, if you want. Or I'll take you to get your car and you can go home, to the office, wherever. It's up to you, Holly."

She loosened her death grip on the day planner. Sam relaxed, too, feeling he was making some progress.

"I almost forgot. There's something for you in the cooler," Sam added, nodding toward the insulated six-pack cooler lying partway beneath her feet.

"No, thanks. I had a lot of iced tea back at the—"

"It's not a drink."

"What is it?"

He'd never met a woman harder to give a gift to. "It's nothing sinister, if that's what you're wondering. Just open it, okay?"

It was worth every bit of trouble just to see the look on her face when Holly opened the cooler and pulled the bouquet of yellow black-eyed Susans from inside.

"If you're trying to soften me up with flowers, Sam McKenzie, I'm afraid you're succeeding," she smiled.

"The florist kept aiming me toward the other kinds of flowers, but you looked like a daisy kind of girl to me—the kind of girl who doesn't need fancy packaging to know what she likes."

He glanced at her, at a loss to explain it any better than that. She was still smiling, looking flushed and surprised, and Sam had a sudden image of Holly as a little girl. Her red hair was in two pigtails instead of the businesslike layered haircut she had now, and she had a sprinkling of freckles over her nose. If they had a little girl someday, she'd probably have freckles, too.

Whoa. Sam slapped the brakes on that idea in a hurry, shaking his head to clear it.

Returning to the matter at hand, Sam said, "Now that you've been kidnapped from the golf course and duly softened up, what do you want to do? Go to the zoo, to the mountains? The county fair's going on. We could even—" he paused for dramatic effect "—go bowling."

"Bowling?"

They both laughed.

"Fun is all in how you look at it," he protested. "With the right attitude, anything can be fun. I'm going to see that you have a whole day of nothing but fun."

At the stoplight, Sam glanced over at her. Holly looked back at him, worriedly biting her lower lip. "I really ought to go back in to work . . ." she objected halfheartedly.

"Come on, it'll be fun. You look like you could use some cheering up, anyway. Weren't things going very well with Brad back there?"

"What makes you say that?"

"Just a feeling." And the way she'd looked so miserable standing next to the guy. "What do you say?"

She took a deep breath. "First there's something I've got to know."

That sounded ominous. "What is it?"

Holly lifted her flowers. "Did you really mean to put these on ice?"

Sam laughed. "Yeah—I was afraid they'd get wilted."

"Good. In that case, maybe you're not as crazy as you seem after all. Let's go."

Chapter Six

They went to the county fair. Standing beside Sam as she had her hand ink-stamped by the attendant, Holly could see why he had suggested it. It was the perfect place for a boy in a grown man's body like Sam McKenzie.

He took her hand and they walked inside the fenced fairground together, shoulders nearly touching. It felt surprisingly natural to be so close to Sam. As long as she was being spontaneous again, Holly decided, she might as well throw herself into the experience. She gave Sam's hand a squeeze.

He smiled down at her. "Better than golfing?"

Holly nodded. "What should we do first?"

"Eat," he said decisively.

"Eat? It's not even dinner time."

"You do everything by the clock?"

"No, but . . . quit shaking your head at me. What's wrong with having a regular schedule?" Holly protested.

"Nothing," Sam replied, giving her a goofy, smiling look she couldn't quite decipher. "There's nothing wrong with it. But I don't think my stomach's on your schedule yet. Come on."

He made a beeline for the hot dog vendor, an umbrella-topped wagon where the hot dogs spun around endlessly on a revolving rotisserie. Every time the vendor opened the rotisserie door, the scent of roasted hot dogs wafted into the air. Holly's stomach growled.

"It's on me," Sam said, pulling some money from his wallet. "What would you like?"

Holly hesitated, watching in appalled fascination as the vendor plopped a hot dog into a split bun and began piling on ketchup, mustard, relish—every condiment in the array before him. She wouldn't have thought so much could fit atop a single hot dog.

"I'm not sure," Holly said. "Why don't you go ahead and order while I decide?"

"Okay." Turning to the vendor, Sam ordered two hot dogs with everything and a root beer.

The gray-haired vendor started on Sam's order, then paused, spoon in midair. "Chili?"

"On both, thanks." Sam looked at Holly. "Anything look good to you?"

She looked at the hot dogs again. "Well . . . yes, but—"

Holly waved for the vendor's attention. "Excuse me, but can you tell me what those are made of, please?" she asked him. He stared at her as though she'd just started speaking Japanese.

"I mean, are they all-beef hot dogs? Or turkey? Or . . . what?"

Holly's voice trailed off. Now Sam was looking at her funny, too.

"They're just hot dogs, lady," replied the vendor. "You want one or not?"

"Ummm . . ." She couldn't decide. Holly was starving, but did she really want to eat something she couldn't identify—or worse, something that was almost pure saturated fat? It wouldn't be smart. If she got fat, she wouldn't stand a chance of winning Brad back with her Plan. Brad disliked women who let themselves go.

"Is this another MSG reaction thing?" Sam asked. "Or is it something else? We can go to another vendor if you want."

"Is this kind of stuff all you ever eat?" Holly asked him, wondering how he'd managed to get so big on what seemed to be an exclusive diet of pizza, mysterious Chinese food, donuts, coffee, and hot dogs.

He shrugged. "Never thought about it much."

She'd have to show Sam how to cook himself a decent meal before the summer was through. At the rate he was going, he'd keel over from a cholesterol overdose by the time he was thirty-five. He needed somebody to watch out for him. He need taking care of.

Whoa. Maybe he did, but she wouldn't be the one who did it. Had she time-warped into the Fifties or something? Holly Aldridge had bigger goals than taking care of a husband.

Double whoa. Husband? She didn't know where *that* came from. Holly steered her attention back to the hot dogs and tried to think spontaneously.

"Well, lady?" The hot dog vendor stared impatiently at her. Behind her the line of people waiting was growing.

"Would you rather go someplace else?" Sam asked.

Holly made her decision. "No. Never mind what's in it. I'll take one . . . with everything, please. And a root beer, too."

Being spontaneous was starting to feel awfully good.

So was indulging her appetite, Holly decided as she licked the last of the chili from her fingertips minutes later. It was worth the extra time she'd have to spend working it off on the stairmaster tomorrow. Holly sipped the foamy remnants of her root beer through her straw and glanced over at Sam.

He was watching her. "Good?"

"Mmm-hmm. I can't remember the last time I ate a hot dog. I ought to get up and walk it off," she confessed, "but I'm just too comfortable to move right away."

She patted the picnic bench they were sitting on and smiled at him. "This is nice. You really know how to treat a girl, Sam."

He gave her a wary look.

Holly laughed and waved her arm at their surroundings—a grassy spot near the exhibition hall shaded by two mesquite trees. "No, really! I mean it. It's peaceful here, and it's nice not to have to worry about impressing anybody for a change."

"Thanks—I think."

Sam ducked his head and finished the last bite of his hot dog. When he looked up again, one corner of his lips was decorated with a little smear of chili.

"Umm, you've got a little bit of chili,"—Holly tapped her fingertip at the corner of her lips—"right here."

"Here?" He probed one corner with the tip of his tongue.

"Other side."

He tried again.

"No, lower. Here—wait a minute." Grabbing a clean napkin from the pile on Sam's lap, she moved closer to him and wiped away the spot. Beneath her fingertip, the corner of his mouth raised in a smile.

"There. I got it," she said, dabbing at the other side for good measure. "I guess nobody could eat with as much gusto as you do and not make a mess occasionally."

"Thanks."

Holly lowered her hand and made herself stop looking at Sam's lips. Her gaze settled somewhere between his shoulder and jaw.

"You need a shave," she informed him, trying to keep up her end of the conversation. The air practically vibrated between them. She needed to get back on safer ground, but before Holly could slide away, Sam wrapped his arms around her waist.

"I know," he said. The tone of his voice made it plain he couldn't care less about razor stubble.

He was looking at her; she felt it. Holly risked a glance back at him. Her stupid, traitorous gaze went straight to his mouth again. They were close enough to share the same breath. Close enough to know better.

"Unless you want to be kissed again," Sam warned, "you'd better quit looking at me like that."

"Like what?"

"Like I'm an especially tasty morsel of something you stopped indulging in a long, long time ago."

Holly took a deep breath. "Maybe it's time to stop denying myself," she said slowly, assessing the dark shadow of beard stubble on his jaw. What would it feel like if she rubbed her cheek across it, just a little?

"Maybe," Sam agreed.

That brought her up short. "You sound like you don't

care one way or the other." Didn't he want to kiss her again? Was she so lousy at it the last time? Wasn't he even going to try to encourage her?

"I care." He smiled, wryly. "Do it then."

Their eyes met. She couldn't breathe, couldn't move. Her spontaneity dissolved beneath the intensity of his expression, taking her bravado with it. This was real. No amount of rationalizing could change that.

"But do it because you want to," Sam said, his voice lowered, "and not for any other reason. Not because you're mad at your boyfriend or you want to prove something to me. Not because I kissed you first,"—he smiled at that—"but just because you want to."

No excuses. Holly could recognize a warning when she heard one. This one should've doused her feelings like a bucket of ice water, but it didn't. Her whole body tensed with anticipation. Yes, yes—it had been so long. "Yes," she whispered. "I . . . I do want to."

Sam cupped her cheek in his hand, his fingertips stroking slowly beneath her ear. "Look at me, then. Look at me and know the man you're with."

It was Sam. Scruffy, messy, love-at-first-sight Sam, and in the instant before her eyes drifted closed, he was the sexiest man she'd ever seen. She kissed him.

It was the most potent experience she could remember having. As soon as she opened her eyes again, Holly knew she'd been crazy to think one taste was enough. Being with Sam made her want to throw common sense to the wind.

She shot to the other side of the bench like her behind was on fire. "So, what should we do next?" Holly asked, wishing her voice would quit shaking.

Sam leaned his head against the bench, looking over at her with half-closed eyes. "More kissing?"

Holly shook her head. "No."

"No?"

"No," she said firmly. "Besides, anybody could see us here."

"You won't kiss me because somebody might see." It wasn't a question.

"That's right," she lied. "Wasn't once enough for you?"

"Not nearly." He ran his fingertips along the bare skin of her upper arm, raising a shivery trail of goose bumps. "Was it enough for you?"

"I have a fiancé . . . at least, I think I still do. I shouldn't even be here." Holly got up, grabbed her day planner and purse, and dug out her sunglasses. Looking at him through their dark lenses, she said, "Maybe you should just take me home."

"I'm not going to force myself on you, Holly."

"I know."

Sam reached for her hand. "Scared?"

Yes. Scared of you, scared of me. Scared of losing my best chance at happiness. She couldn't say it out loud.

"Should I be?" Holly asked instead. It sounded ridiculous even to herself. She tried again. "I'm sorry, Sam. The kiss was a mistake. Things didn't work out for me with Brad today, and I guess I was feeling vulnerable. I won't let it happen again. It wouldn't be fair to anyone."

Sam crumpled his paper cup and threw it into the trash can, then he turned to face her.

"Okay," he said. "I understand."

Holly wasn't sure what to expect, but it wasn't what she heard next: "Want to hit some rides before we go?"

Saturday night. Date night—at least for the happily coupled half of the planet's population. Standing alone in the vestibule of Francie's restaurant, Holly felt decidedly in the un-coupled half. She turned her back on the lovebird couples waiting for tables and hugged the phone tighter in the nook between her ear and shoulder. She played with the cold metal phone cord, listening to the impersonal ringing on the other end.

Please be home. Come on.

Clarissa answered on the third ring.

"Hi, it's me," Holly said, trying to sound upbeat. "You busy?"

"What's wrong?"

"Nothing. I—" God, Clarissa always knew when something was wrong, even when Holly tried to hide it. Her throat tightened, making it hard to speak. She blinked, staring hard at the battered, graffiti-covered yellow pages swinging on the chain beneath the pay phone. It helped distract her long enough to finish talking. "You want to catch a movie or something?"

Silence. Holly could picture the scene, though—Clarissa sitting cross-legged on her black kitchen countertop, phone cradled to her ear, probably painting her toenails orange. Clarissa was big on beauty rituals.

"Sure," Clarissa said. "A movie movie, or a video rental?"

Saturday night. Date night—the movie theater would be packed with hand-holding, smiling couples. The kind of couple Holly wasn't part of anymore.

"A video."

"Gotcha. I'll meet you at your place in half an hour."

"Unless . . . unless you've got other plans. With David, I mean. I don't want to interrupt anything."

"Don't be silly, Holly. Get yourself home—and be careful, too."

"Yes, Mom," Holly said, smiling for the first time in what felt like hours. "See you then."

When Holly pulled into her driveway at home, Sam's truck was nowhere in sight. He was probably out on a date, too—so much for love at first sight. He'd left the porch light on for her, though. She trudged up the sidewalk to the front porch, then kicked off her high heels and sat on the porch swing beside Sam's potted barrel cactus.

The little spiky plant had taken up permanent residence on the swing, where it got plenty of sunshine during the day. Cradling its terra-cotta pot with one hand to keep it steady, Holly dug her stockinged toes into the porch floorboards and set the swing in motion.

Things weren't turning out the way she wanted them. The worst part was, Holly couldn't figure out why. Everything ought to be peachy. You study hard, you get straight A's. You work hard, you get promoted. You find the right man, you get loved. Except she'd found the right man, and Brad didn't love her. He was messing up the rest of the equation. Where was the happily-ever-after ending?

Not that she was naïve enough to believe all relationships ended happily. Her divorced parents were proof of that. But their marriage had begun in the heat of passion; it would've been impossible to sustain that, wouldn't it? In contrast, with Brad Holly had found a man with a background, interests, and professional goals that were all similar to hers. It should've at least increased her odds of success.

Instead it only left her feeling lonely.

Headlights brightened the porch as Clarissa's teal-colored sports car pulled into the driveway and roared to a stop. Clarissa got out and tromped up the walk carrying an overflowing department store shopping bag.

"Hey, what are you doing out here?" she asked.

Holly stopped the swing. Clarissa picked up the cactus and settled herself in its place, balancing the pot on her bare knees. She plunked her shopping bag between them, and they started swinging again.

"I'm just thinking about stuff," Holly said. "I haven't made it inside yet."

She hadn't wanted to go in alone. Weeknights were easier; Holly could stay at work late, and tell herself she was being productive. There were no such excuses on the weekend. The empty house waited for her, a big old reminder of how empty her life was becoming, too.

Clarissa tapped the shopping bag. "I've got all the essentials in here. A couple of Charlie Chaplin movies and some microwave popcorn if you're feeling happy, *Casablanca* and a jumbo box of tissues if you're not, and two pints of fudge ripple in either case." She smiled sympathetically. "Plus a good ear for listening. What'll it be?"

Holly burst into tears.

Clarissa stopped the swing. "I knew I should've brought a Mel Gibson movie, too. Mel's good for all occasions." She dug into the bag and pressed a wad of tissues into Holly's hand.

"Do you want to tell me what happened? Or should I just go wring Brad's neck right now? You did go to dinner with him tonight at Francie's like you planned, right?"

Holly nodded, sniffling.

"He stood you up. Damn him!"

"No . . . no, he didn't stand me up. He was there." Holly blew her nose and tried to get herself under control. Her nose was so plugged up she sounded like a Muppet when she talked.

"He was there, but he was a half hour late," she continued. "Gina—his secretary—called the restaurant to let me know, otherwise I probably would've left."

Yeah, right—she would've stayed out of pure stubbornness, if nothing else. Determination had served her well over the past few years. Holly couldn't admit that to Clarissa, though. She still had *some* pride left.

"How did his secretary know about your romantic dinner together?"

"I made the plans through her. You know how busy Brad is."

Clarissa shook her head. "I still think you should've left. It would've served him right."

"I'm not trying to teach him a lesson. I'm trying to put our relationship back on track again." Holly sighed. It was starting to look like she was the only one interested in keeping things going between them.

Clarissa pulled two diet colas from the depths of her bag and cracked one open for each of them. "Negates the calories to come later from the fudge ripple," she said, winking. "So Brad the Bad strolls in late. Then what?"

"Well, he joined me at the table, our special table—*The Table*—where we sat on our first date."

Their first date, Holly's first blind date. Her mother had fixed her up with Brad, after meeting him the day she'd closed the sale of his parents' new half-million-dollar Arizona vacation home.

"Uh-huh. Good move, the special table," Clarissa said. "Part of the emotional appeal phase of your Plan?"

"Yes." Holly was a little surprised Clarissa remembered

the Plan so well. "But Brad didn't like it. He spent the first ten minutes badgering the waiter into seating us further from the kitchen." Holly sighed, remembering. "The poor waiter didn't know what to do. I'd slipped him five bucks to seat us there."

Clarissa tilted her head back, staring up at the white porch roof. "Men can be so clueless about sentimental things," she said. "David still thinks I picked red roses for our wedding because they matched the bridesmaid's dresses best. Duh! They were the first kind of flowers he ever gave me."

Holly's mind flashed on the bunch of yellow black-eyed Susans Sam had given her the day of the county fair. Good thing she wasn't marrying Sam—they'd make a pretty goofy wedding bouquet.

"I know," Holly said. "I don't think they can help it."

She swigged some diet cola, then remembered the fudge ripple ice cream in Clarissa's bag. "Do you want to put the ice cream in the freezer?"

Clarissa carried her shopping bag inside and Holly followed, swinging her sleek new black shoes by their ankle straps. She didn't know why she'd bothered getting dressed up. Brad hadn't looked at her twice throughout the whole meal. If not for his perfunctory, "You look nice tonight, Holly," she'd have thought he hadn't noticed her efforts at all.

"The fudge ripple's safely stowed for later," Clarissa said when she came back into the living room. She flopped down next to Holly on the sofa and sat hugging her knees to her chest. "So tell me the rest. What happened after Brad finished browbeating the waiter?"

"Well, we ordered dinner." Holly paused, squinting as though it would help her remember clearly. "You know," she said, "I always thought it was so charming of Brad to order for me when we went out someplace. But tonight . . . I don't know, it seemed a little . . ."

She stopped and shook her head. "I'm probably just mad because things didn't work out. But I didn't like it. And it wasn't just that, either. I can't really put my finger on it. It was as if Brad wasn't really *there,* you know what I mean?"

Clarissa nodded, setting her soda can on the glass coffee table top. Holly automatically reached for a coaster, then stopped. That was Brad's rule, not hers. Whose house was it, anyway?

"I know what you mean," Clarissa said, grinning. "David's like that if I try to talk to him while he's watching ESPN. Zombie man. Not all there."

"Exactly. Brad kept looking around, like he was looking for someone." *Or looking for an escape route.* "I had it all planned out," Holly went on. "I brought a portable CD player along so I could play our favorite song. I brought pictures of the ski trip we took last December, so we could reminisce about the good times. I even alluded to the first time we, ahh . . ."

"Did the deed?" Clarissa suggested with a wicked lift of her eyebrows.

"Noodled. Brad called it noodling."

"What?"

"It's true," Holly admitted, feeling herself flush. "Whenever Brad was, ummm, in the mood, he'd kind of nudge me and say, 'Want some noodling, little girl?'"

"Gross!"

"I guess it does sound a little strange. I got used to it."

Clarissa gave her a sympathetic look. Holly shrugged.

"Anyway, nothing worked tonight. Brad didn't want to reminisce. He said playing our song would disturb the other diners, and he flipped through the vacation pictures like they'd catch fire if he held onto them longer than two seconds apiece."

Tears of frustration welled in her eyes. "What am I doing wrong, Clarissa? I'm really trying here, but I must be doing something wrong, 'cause it's not working!"

"It's not you, hon," Clarissa said soothingly, patting Holly's upper arm. "It's Brad the Bad. Honest. It's got to be."

Clarissa paused. "Have you ever considered he's just not the right man for you?"

"No. Uh-uh." Feeling a need to keep busy, Holly reached for Clarissa's shopping bag and dug around in it. She pulled out the videos and plopped all three onto the coffee table.

"I can't give up now, not after everything I've already invested in this relationship," she explained. "What if I'm almost there? What if I just need a little more time before Brad realizes we belong together? We were really great together once."

"Once? What about right now? What about cutting your losses and moving on?" Clarissa insisted. "You deserve better than this."

"I can't just give up. Not yet, at least."

Clarissa threw both hands in the air. "But it's not all up to you. Maybe you've done all you can already."

Holly thought about the lingerie squashed in her bottom bureau drawer, still in its potpourri-scented bag. "Not quite everything," she said. "There's still phase three of the Plan."

Groaning, Clarissa stretched her arm toward the shopping bag and dragged it across the polished oak floorboards. "You mean the seduction routine," she said, her voice muffled because she was searching for something in the bag. "I didn't think it would come to that."

That was heartening. It must mean Clarissa thought she'd have convinced Brad to come back long before this. "I didn't, either," Holly replied. "It's my last resort."

"Oh, boy. I need more fortification for this," Clarissa said.

She ripped the cellophane wrapper from the box of microwave popcorn she'd brought, and crumpled it noisily in her hand. Holly followed her to the microwave, still talking:

"I think it'll work, though. The seduction thing, that is."

"Hmmph."

"Well, aren't they always saying men think with their . . ." Holly gestured vaguely, then swallowed hard. "You know."

Raising her eyebrows, Clarissa said, "Their . . . ?"

"*You* know." Holly gave her hips a little swivel, got even more embarrassed, and shut up.

"You can't even say it, can you?"

"I just don't want to."

Clamping her lips together, Holly stared at the popcorn as it spun, popping noisily, on the microwave's carousel. When it was finished she pulled out the hot popcorn bag with her fingertips and devoted all her attention to ripping the edges apart. Salty popcorn-scented steam billowed upward.

"You can't say it," Clarissa said. "Admit it."

"No."

Holly dumped the popcorn into a green glass bowl and hurried into the living room with her head held high. Clarissa followed her like a little yappy dog.

"Jeez, are you ever repressed," she said. "I had no idea. Come on, say it. I won't tell anybody." She was smiling now, holding back a laugh. She poked Holly's shoulder. "It's okay, you know. You're a grown woman, you're supposed to know about this stuff. Didn't your mother ever talk to you?"

She flipped a piece of popcorn into her mouth, crunching it while she waited for Holly to speak. Before Holly could get a word out, though, Clarissa held up both hands.

"No, wait. I don't think I want to know what your mother, the ice queen, told you," she said, shuddering in mock horror.

"Ha, ha. My point was," Holly said laboriously, "that I think sex appeal would work on most men, Brad included."

Clarissa—her friend, her best friend since ninth grade—snorted. Holly threw a piece of popcorn at her.

Ducking, Clarissa asked, "What about Sam?"

"He's a perfect example of my theory," Holly declared, feeling smug. "Sam practically sweats sex appeal—"

"Ewww."

"Okay, bad word choice." Holly thought about it some more. "What I mean is, he's totally centered in the here and now. The man lives like there's no tomorrow. He eats what he wants, wears what he wants . . . Sam takes what he wants," she added, remembering the feel of his body pressing into hers. *Feel, feel us together, feel me.*

A shiver passed through her. "Sam's definitely a man who thinks with his you-know-what," she concluded. "And I'll bet he's pretty typical." *Liar,* a part of her whispered. *He's anything but typical.*

Clarissa shook her head. "Sam is in love with you."

"Sam only thinks he's in love with me," Holly disagreed. "That's infatuation. There's a big difference. That kind of love can't last."

Looking sober, Clarissa pushed away the popcorn bowl and wiped her fingers on a napkin. "It might, Holly. And if it did, it would be the greatest kind of love there is."

Holly sighed and picked up *Casablanca,* slipping the videocassette from its case. "That kind of love only happens in the movies," she said as she inserted the tape into the VCR. "Only in the movies."

Chapter Seven

The next morning dawned bright and sunny and much too early for someone who'd slept as poorly as Holly had. She rolled over in bed, whacked the snooze button on her clock radio, and dragged a pillow over her face. Why in the world had she set the alarm for seven-thirty on a Sunday morning?

Because she'd invited her mother, along with Clarissa and her husband David, over for brunch, that's why. Groaning, Holly pulled her cheery floral comforter over her head. After her disastrous evening with Brad, hosting a brunch party fell someplace below having a bikini wax on her list of Things to Look Forward To.

Snap out of it. It'll probably be fun, Holly told herself as she crawled out from beneath her comforter cave. She pulled on a pair of old shorts beneath the soft cotton T-shirt she slept in—no sense ruining her nice clothes by cooking brunch in them—and headed for the kitchen to get started.

Forty-five minutes before everyone was due to arrive, Sam ambled barefoot into the kitchen wearing nothing but a pair of plaid boxer shorts and a groggy smile.

"Morning. You look busy," he remarked as he poured himself a cup of black coffee.

"You look like you just got up," Holly replied, eyeing his rumpled hair and unshaven jaw. The rest of him she tried to ignore, but it wasn't easy. The man sure looked good wearing mostly skin and a smile. "It's after ten already."

"I know. I was out kind of late last night." He blew on his coffee and then sipped. "Ahh—that hits the spot."

Holly didn't doubt it. It had been after one o'clock when she'd finally heard Sam come home. Not that she'd been specifically listening for him, or anything—it was probably just a coincidence that she was still awake finishing the last of the fudge ripple when his key turned in the lock.

"Did you have a good time?" *Wherever you were?*

"Yeah." He squinted into the distance and didn't say anything else. Poor Sam was a slow starter in the morning; probably the caffeine hadn't reached his brain yet. Holly didn't know how he managed to get up at such an ungodly hour to work construction every day.

He blinked, downed the rest of his coffee, and looked around the kitchen. "Quite a production. Are you expecting company, or are you just especially hungry today?"

"Did I forget to tell you?" Holly maneuvered around him and picked up the basket of strawberries she'd bought to go with the French toast she was making. "I invited Clarissa and David—and my mother—over for brunch this morning."

"I'm not invited?"

"Sure you are—if you really want to join us." Holly

made a face. "I just thought I'd spare you the ordeal of meeting my mother."

Sam remained silent. Holly sliced away the green top of a fat strawberry with surgical precision, not looking at him. He wasn't buying it, she could tell.

"My mother can be pretty hard to take sometimes," Holly added by way of explanation. *You big chicken,* her conscience jabbed, but it was already too late. "Clarissa and David are used to her by now, but . . ."

"But I'm not."

"Right." Holly stemmed the strawberries faster, weak with cowardly relief when Sam left her to pour another cup of coffee. He came back and put his hand around hers, taking the paring knife from her grip.

"You're going to slice more than the strawberries if you keep that up," he said, gently bumping her aside with his hip so he could reach the green plastic berry basket. "I'll finish this. It looks like you've got a lot to do."

It was worse than she'd thought. Sam was going to be nice about being excluded from the brunch party, despite the lame excuse she'd given him. Nobody's mother was so difficult to deal with as to be unmeetable. Well, Holly's probably came close. Still, it would've been easier if Sam had gotten mad instead.

Holly took a clear glass pitcher from the cupboard and poured in the orange juice she'd defrosted. "This Sunday brunch is kind of a regular thing," she said. "My mother's been out of town the last couple of weeks, so we haven't been able to get together for a while."

Holly had hoped to avoid a meeting between her mother and Sam even longer. Forever would've been nice. If her mother met Sam—her new roommate—then Holly would have to explain what had happened between her and Brad. Her mother would be so disappointed.

"Business travel or pleasure?" Sam asked, handing her the bowl of sliced strawberries. "Tell me this workaholic thing doesn't run in the family. Or do all of you work a billion hours a week?"

He popped a hulled strawberry in her mouth. Surprised,

Holly chewed. When she finished, she said, "I don't work a billion hours a week."

Brad had never pestered her about how much she worked—he was exactly the same way. Maybe that was why they were so well suited for each other. Of course, that might turn into a problem when they had a family together someday, but ... but she'd deal with that when it happened.

Sam raised his eyebrows, still waiting for her answer.

"It was business," Holly admitted. "A broker's conference. My mother's a real-estate broker. A good one, too—she's a million-dollar producer."

He nodded, looking suitably impressed. "What does your Dad do?"

"He's a plumber—at least he was the last time I talked to him. He's lived in Montana ever since the divorce. I haven't seen him for a while."

Holly sprinkled sugar on the strawberries and shoved the bowl into the refrigerator. She shut the door, turned around, and ran smack into Sam's chest. He handed her the juice pitcher.

"I finished the orange juice."

"See, you *can* cook!"

"Only under pressure." Holly put both hands around the cold glass pitcher, but he didn't release it. She had to look up at him. "The divorce must've been hard," Sam said. "How old were you?"

"When they got divorced? About ten, I guess." Exactly ten; they'd announced it the morning after her birthday slumber party. "Can I have the juice, please?"

Sam handed it over. "Don't want to talk about it?"

"No. Yes. No." Holly swung the refrigerator door closed with her hip and hurried past him. "I've just got a lot to do, that's all. I still need to get dressed, and I haven't even started the French toast yet."

"Can I help?" he asked.

"You know," Holly went on blithely, "I don't have any hidden traumas over my parent's divorce, if that's what you're thinking. Lots of people get divorced."

She grabbed a sauté pan from the cupboard and plopped slices of Canadian bacon into it to warm. Waggling the empty package at Sam, she added, "In fact, *most* people get divorced. Did you ever think of that?"

He took away the bacon wrapper and tossed it into the trash. Holly couldn't believe she'd actually waved it at him like a shrewish wife on a TV sitcom. She was losing it.

Sam rubbed her shoulders like she was a boxer going into the ring. "Tell me what to do and I'll help you," he said patiently.

She didn't deserve such kind treatment, not when she was purposely trying to hide him from her mother. Well, not hide him exactly—it wasn't like she was embarrassed about Sam. Holly only wanted to . . . delay all the explanations for a while.

"It would probably be safe to let me get the stuff out for your French toast," he offered, still rubbing her shoulders.

His hands felt really good. Holly hadn't realized she was so tense. It wasn't even noon yet. It ought to be illegal to feel tense before noon. "It's nice of you to offer, Sam, but you don't have to help. Really. I can do it."

"I know that. I want to. Where's the bread? In the cupboard?"

He took his hands away and headed for the row of cupboards above the sink. Holly glanced at the clock again, feeling like a sprinter at the starting line of the race. They'd be here any minute. She couldn't resist any longer. If Sam was going to insist on helping her she'd just have to let him, however rotten a person it made her seem.

"It's right there in the—"

"In the . . . ?"

"In the grocery store!" Holly grabbed him. "Oh, no—I forgot to buy the bread! How am I going to make French toast without bread?"

The doorbell chimed. Great—somebody was early, and Holly would lay odds it was her mother. She stared toward the living room, frozen. So did Sam.

"You want me to get that while you go change?"

Holly looked down at his naked chest, dark cotton boxer

shorts, and bare feet. A burble of hysterical laughter stuck in her throat. "My mother would have a heart attack if you answered my front door looking like that."

Ding . . . DING!

"Okay," Sam said. "I've got a plan. I'll get dressed, go buy a loaf of bread, and sneak it back in. Nobody will ever know."

Holly was desperate. She nodded.

"Cover me." Grinning, Sam ducked so he wouldn't be seen from the windows overlooking the front porch and headed toward his bedroom. Once he'd vanished down the hallway, Holly decided it was safe to open the door.

"Mom!"

"Hi, sweetie." Linda Aldridge dropped her cigarette and crushed it beneath the two-inch curved heel of her navy spectator pumps, then came inside. Smiling, she enveloped her daughter in a Giorgio-scented, bracelet-clinking hug. "I hope I'm not too early."

"Maybe just a few minutes," Holly replied, smiling apologetically. Somehow she never felt quite ready for her mother. Out of the corner of her eye, she saw Sam's head peek around the hallway corner. Holly frantically waved him back.

Her mother glanced down at Holly's shorts and T-shirt. "It must be so liberating not to feel like you have to get all fixed up for company," her mother remarked. "You girls all look so wonderfully casual these days."

Loosely translated, *whatever possessed you to put that pile of rags on?* Holly glanced down, too.

"I haven't had a chance to change yet. I'll just be a minute, Mom—why don't you help yourself to a cup of coffee while you wait?"

"Nonsense. I'll help with brunch."

Her mother headed for the kitchen, leaving Holly staring at her impeccably dressed back. There was a series of thumps—her briefcase, cigarette case, and cellular phone hitting the countertop—then she called, "You're lucky I got here before the rest of your guests. It looks as though you still have a lot to do."

Holly hurried to the hallway. "The coast's clear," she whispered to Sam, grabbing a handful of his sleeve to urge him into the living room. They got partway to the front door before the click-click of her mother's heels on the kitchen linoleum stopped them. Holly shoved Sam back into the hallway just as her mother appeared beneath the kitchen archway.

"Didn't you hear me? I was wondering what you want me to do with this?" She held out a sauté pan filled with shrunken, black, inedible-looking disks. They were still sizzling.

Holly leaned against the hallway arch, blocking it with her body. "Err . . . throw it out, I guess. It used to be the Canadian bacon," she answered.

Sam whispered, "I'll get bacon, too."

"*Shhh,*" she hissed under her breath. She smiled at her mother, spreading her arms wider in case Sam was peeking around the corner again. "I think I've got more someplace. I'll, umm . . . be right there to help, okay?"

Wrinkling her nose, Linda returned to the kitchen. Holly ducked into the hall and grabbed Sam's sleeve. "Hurry— now's your chance."

He leaned there against the wall for a second, looking almost like he was enjoying himself, his arms crossed.

"You look wonderfully casual to me, too," he mimicked, grinning down at her shorts and T-shirt. Holly remembered she wasn't even wearing a bra, never mind nice clothes. She clapped her hands over her chest.

Sam pulled her toward him and gave her a fast kiss. "Back in a minute," he said, and was gone before she could say a word.

Fifteen minutes later Sam hadn't returned and Holly was on the verge of strangling her mother with Linda's designer silk scarf. So far her mother had offered advice on how to best scramble eggs, brew coffee, decorate her kitchen, and choose a car insurance company. She was in the middle of writing the name of a good hairdresser on the back of one of her business cards when the doorbell rang.

"Sorry, got to get that," Holly said, all but running to the doorway to let Clarissa and David in.

It was Sam.

"What are you doing ringing the doorbell?" Holly whispered, looking frantically toward the kitchen. Her mother, thankfully oblivious to them, was humming and rearranging the place settings on the banquette table. Holly went outside and closed the door behind her. She stood nose to chest with Sam on the front porch.

"Would you believe I'm the grocery delivery boy? You can just tip me whatever you think my services are worth." Sam winked, lifting the brown paper sack in his arms.

Holly didn't feel much like kidding around. "What if my mother had answered the door and seen all those groceries?"

"What if she had?"

"She'd have known I can't even manage brunch for four people, that's what," she said, grabbing for the sack.

Sam held on to it. "So? She's your mom, not an entertainment critic. She's not going to care if you forgot the bread."

"You don't know my mother." Holly stopped and took a deep, calming breath. "Thanks for getting this."

"You're welcome. Need anything else?"

"Yes—just once I need to have my mother *not* criticizing everything I do," she said. "Kidding," she added upon seeing the look on Sam's face. "She's not that bad. What I really need is to get this stuff inside without being seen."

Holly thought about it for a second. "I'll go inside and get her away from the kitchen somehow. Just give me a minute or two, then bring everything inside, okay?"

Sam squinted at her, probably wishing he'd had more coffee before being forced to deal with her family. "Are you sure this is necessary?"

She nodded. "Thanks, Sam. You don't know what this means to me," she said, then she went back inside.

* * *

Sam had a pretty good idea what it meant to her, despite wishing he didn't. After hearing Holly's conversation with her mother, he was starting to understand why she was so persnickety about everything. She was trying to make everything she did mistake-proof. Trying to get the jump on her mother's constant criticism.

Shouldering the grocery sack, Sam counted to one hundred, then cautiously opened the front door. All clear. He started toward the kitchen. Halfway there, the doorbell chimed loudly enough to make his left eardrum go numb.

He was standing right beneath the old-fashioned doorbell chimes mounted near the ceiling. Sam went to the door and whipped it open.

Clarissa and David looked at him, then at the sack he was holding. "Is that a door prize?" Clarissa asked with a teasing grin, "or did Holly finally kick you out for leaving your socks in the refrigerator one too many times?"

David chuckled. He and Clarissa were a perfect match—he actually seemed to think her jokes were funny.

"It was just that one time," Sam said. "I set them down while I was getting a beer."

"Mmm-hmm."

He couldn't believe Holly had actually told someone about the sock incident.

"Get used to it, Sam," David put in. "I don't have any secrets left."

"Holly really told you about that?"

"Holly tells me *all* about you." Clarissa sauntered inside, sniffing. "Is Holly's mom here already? I thought I smelled that ritzy perfume of hers when we were coming up the walk."

"She's here all right." Sam carried the groceries into the kitchen. Clarissa and David followed. "And she's making Holly crazy."

"That's what mothers are for," said an evenly modulated voice behind him. Holly's mother, Sam assumed.

They all turned to face Linda Aldridge, standing quietly on the other side of the built-in bar. She looked like an older, brittler version of Holly with auburn helmet hair, a lot of careful makeup, and a slick business suit. She said hello to Clarissa and David, then smiled and walked around the bar to meet Sam.

"Isn't it a mother's job to watch out for her child?" she asked, offering him a bejeweled handshake—and a quick once-over. "I don't think we've met. I'm Linda, Holly's mother. And you're . . . ?"

Sam's gaze darted behind her, where Holly stood watching. "I'm Sam McKenzie. Clarissa's cousin," he said, juggling the grocery sack to accept her handshake. "Hope you don't mind me crashing the party. I offered to . . . ah, cook."

Holly's eyes widened. She started shaking her head.

"Now isn't that enlightened? It's nice to meet you, Stan."

"Sam."

"Of course, silly me." Linda put both hands together and tilted her head. "Why don't we all go in the other room and give Sam room to work?" she suggested.

"He's not the caterer, Mom."

"Oh."

Sam bit back a grin. Now he understood why Holly was concerned about being dressed-up enough for her mother's visit.

Holly hesitated. "Are you sure you don't want some help, Sam?" she asked. *Please let me help*, her expression said.

Sam shook his head. The least he could do was let Holly off the hook in case the French toast tasted like soggy cardboard and wrecked her brunch party. "Leave it all up to me."

The women—except for Holly—beamed at him. "I think it'll be nice to be catered to by a man, for a change," Linda said, smiling. Clarissa agreed. Holly groaned.

"You ladies go on," David put in with a subtle lift of his chest. "We men will take care of you."

Sam didn't want to raise expectations too high, so he only smiled encouragingly. Once the women had disappeared into the living room, he turned to David. And gave him a shove.

"Are you nuts? 'We *men* will take care of you?'" He smacked his hand on his forehead, then winced. "I've got the hangover of the week—thanks to you, by the way—and you're going on like we're the Galloping Gourmet, here. You ever make French toast before?"

David shrugged. "How hard can it be? I've watched Clarissa do it."

Sam scowled and upended the grocery sack. Two loaves of Wonder bread and a pound of bacon fell onto the countertop. The selection at the mini-market on the corner wasn't the greatest, but it was at least close by.

"As for the hangover," David continued, "I'm not the one who poured all those beers down your throat last night." He gave Sam a sympathetic look. "Did you talk to Holly when you got home, like you said you were going to?"

"No. The timing wasn't right."

It never would be right, as long as Holly was hung up on making things work with Brad. After she'd left for her romantic dinner with him at Francie's, Sam had rambled around for a while in the empty house, trying not to wonder what they were doing together. It took him about five minutes to realize he needed a stronger dose of distraction. Somehow he'd wound up in a bar downtown until after midnight, spilling his guts to David.

"The timing wasn't right?" David shook his head. "You've got to go after what you want, Sam. Grab Holly and make her forget about Brad. Make her yours, man. Tame her!"

Sam rolled his eyes. "She's a woman, not a wild horse. Does Clarissa know about these caveman episodes of yours?"

"Are you kidding? She'd probably kick my ass if she heard me say that." David laughed and took a carton of eggs from the refrigerator. "The point is, Holly and Brad together were about as hot as day-old bread. He treated her more like a roommate than you do, if you catch my drift. Like a business partner. That guy's cold. I don't know why she can't see it."

Sam unwrapped the polka-dotted Wonder bread package and stacked the thin bread slices on a plate. He didn't want to think about Brad the Bad anymore. "Let's just get on with this," he said.

"Besides," David persisted, "they're split. It's just taking Holly a while to catch up. She'll give up sooner or later."

Sam hoped he wouldn't be a gray-haired, arthritic old man by the time that happened. From the living room came the sound of Holly's mother, asking how things were coming in the kitchen.

"Just fine, Mrs. Aldridge," David called. "We'd better get busy," he said, lifting his baseball cap and then ramming it backwards onto his curly black hair.

"You know, now you really *do* look like the Galloping Gourmet."

David cheerfully raised his middle finger in reply. "Stand back," he said, grinning as he cracked eggs into a bowl, "and watch a *real* master at work."

"It's too bad Brad can't be here," Holly's mother said as they all took their places at the banquette table—Clarissa and David on one side, Holly and her mother on the other, Sam perched at the end—and dug into the plates of French toast, strawberries, and bacon.

"He's working," Holly said quickly, crossing her fingers beneath the napkin on her lap. "Maybe he'll be here next time."

Sam shot her a dark look, one she understood better than she wanted to. No matter which way she turned, it seemed she hurt somebody.

"Well," her mother continued, "I wanted to invite you both to my company's annual awards dinner. It's at the Cheshire Hotel downtown, next Saturday night."

Linda chewed a bite of French toast with strawberries, then rested her fork atop her plate. "I've never had anything quite like this, boys," she said.

Holly doubted her mother meant it kindly, but David

smiled at her anyway. "Glad you like it," he said. "Sam deserves most of the credit, though."

Holly helped herself to another piece as a show of loyalty. It tasted a little eggy, but she wanted Sam to know she appreciated his trying to help her.

"I'd love to come to your awards dinner, Mom," she said, "but I'm not sure Brad will be able to make it."

Linda pursed her lips. "I hope he will." She leaned forward and, as an aside to Sam, added, "Brad is Holly's fiancé. A doctor. He always makes *such* a good impression at these events. We're all very proud of him."

Holly sunk a little lower in her seat. Dating Brad was the first thing she'd ever done that her mother actually approved of. How was she going to break it to her if things didn't work out according to her Plan?

"Yes, Brad and I have met," Sam said. "Briefly. He's a busy guy. If Brad can't make it, Holly, I'd be glad to escort you."

Sam was looking straight at her, his eyes so blue and honest she could read his feelings in them. *Be with me.*

"It's a formal business function, dear," her mother put in, frowning. "Don't you think Sam might be a little uncomfortable?" She glanced at him, then hastily away. "I hope this doesn't sound too harsh, but these are professional people who—"

"I don't think Sam would be uncomfortable anyplace," Holly interrupted, still looking at him. "No matter who was there. And come to think of it, I'm just about positive Brad won't be able to make it."

Complete silence descended. All four of them stared at her. Holly's knees starting shaking, and her throat closed up with panic. How was she going to follow up on that? Beneath the table, Sam squeezed her knee. His show of encouragement brought a fresh sting of tears to her eyes, and she had to blink them back before she could go on.

"I'd love it if you escorted me, Sam," Holly blurted out.

Her mother's mouth dropped open. "What will Brad say?"

"He'll probably say he's got to work late," Holly

answered truthfully, "like he usually does." She hoped she wasn't making a stupid, life-changing mistake. Taking a deep breath, she said, "I'd really like to go to your party, Mom, but it'll have to be with Sam."

Thirty seconds later, her mother's voice broke the silence. "If . . . if you insist," she said, sounding bewildered.

Across the table, Clarissa applauded.

Despite her impending date with Sam, Holly wasn't ready to give up on her Plan yet. How else was she going to get her life back to normal again? How else was she going to feel like *herself* again? Holly had even started skipping workouts once a week and leaving work at five o'clock most of the time, all so she could spend more time with Sam. It wasn't like her at all. She needed to re-focus on her goals, Holly decided.

So she spent the next week trying to think up a way to put the final seduction phase of her Plan into motion. Friday night, Brad dropped the solution into her hands by asking her to stop by his office the next morning to evaluate a new accounting software package he was considering for his office. His request couldn't have been more convenient. Even better, the place was usually deserted on the weekend. Late Saturday morning, all systems were go.

Just before noon, Holly drove into the parking lot outside the medical complex that housed Brad's office. She couldn't pull into either of the spaces right next to Brad's shiny BMW, since he'd parked on the line between them, so she parked nearby and turned off the ignition. Her old convertible's engine clattered loudly enough to wake the dead as it gradually wound to a stop.

Wincing at the sound, Holly checked her makeup in the rearview mirror. Tasteful, yet flamboyant enough so Brad would know she wasn't the same old unspontaneous Holly, she decided. Good. She slid her briefcase across the seat. The implements of her mission—the bottles of Lover's Potion and Aphrodisia Massage Oil—clinked together inside. She checked to make sure her garter belt fasteners

SURRENDER 111

were still holding, gave her curled, lightly teased hair one last pat, then got out of the car.

Brad wouldn't know what hit him. The thought made Holly smile as she opened the front door with the key he'd given her long ago, then locked it again behind her. It was now or never.

Dressed only in a belted trench coat with her new lingerie beneath—Clarissa's idea—Holly navigated the wide austere corridors that led to Brad's office. The hallways were chilly. Then again, it was probably perfectly comfortable for people who were dressed. A nervous shiver passed through her. Steeling her resolve, Holly pressed on, the whisper of her stockinged legs sounding unnaturally loud in the deserted building.

Holly breathed a sigh of relief when her key still turned in Brad's office door. Opening it quietly, she tiptoed into the darkened recesses of the suite, where Brad kept his private office. The spike-heeled red shoes Clarissa had talked her into buying made not a whisper of sound on the carpeted floor, but Holly could've sworn her heart was thumping loudly enough to announce her arrival a mile away. And if the hammering of her heart didn't do it, then the aggressively musky perfume she'd dabbed on would give her presence away for sure.

Neither did. Rounding the corner, Holly heard the low-pitched hum of Brad's computer and the tap-tap-tapping of his fingers as he typed. She gripped her briefcase handle tighter, took a deep breath, and approached his open office door.

Her thong panties chose that moment to shoot the rest of the way up her behind.

Holly flung herself back against the wall. A long, agonizing minute passed before she was sure Brad hadn't seen her. Lowering her briefcase gingerly to the floor, she flipped up the back of her tan trench coat and tried to extricate herself from her thong-panty prison.

It was a tricky maneuver, at least when performed on three-inch spike heels. Wavering a little, Holly tugged at the strip of flowered fabric. It stayed in a comfortable position for all of thirty seconds. She might as well have put on the rubber band from the Sunday newspaper, called it underwear, and saved herself seven dollars, for all the luck Holly had getting the thing to stay where it belonged.

She sagged back against the wall to catch her breath. The way things were going, Holly was tempted to just back up, really slowly, and leave.

No. She wasn't giving up yet. Spreading her knees further apart, balancing precariously on her shoes, Holly tightened her grip on the thong. Nervous perspiration trickled between her breasts, dampening the red and black velvet groping-hands bra. Great, that'd make a really sexy impression. Stifling a groan, she gave it another try.

Still holding the panty away from her behind, Holly snapped her knees together again, performed the greatest butt squeeze of her life, and released the thong. The thought crossed her mind that this was probably a pretty good workout—Thongs of Steel. Tight Thongs in Thirty Days. Thong Aerobics.

Oh, boy. Getting hysterical wasn't helping. But she thought the butt squeeze might. Reaching back, Holly gave it one last try, squeezing for all she was worth this time. As long as she stayed clenched, the thong stayed put. Success!

Smiling triumphantly, Holly picked up her briefcase and glanced up. Brad was leaning against the door frame, his arms crossed over his chest, watching her.

"I thought I heard something out here," he said mildly. "I was afraid the cleaning lady was having a heart attack, judging by all the thumping on the wall and the heavy breathing."

He raised his eyebrow—just one, a trick that always irritated her a little because it made him look so superior. Also because she couldn't do it.

"You're late," he said. "I thought you'd changed your mind."

"Are you kidding?" Holly laughed, stepping closer to him. *You can do this. Confidence is sexy,* she told herself. "I'd love to have a look at your, ahh . . . hardware, Brad."

He frowned. "It's software. Didn't I tell you that?"

Jeez, he used to understand innuendo. "That's not what I meant," she said, making her intentions plain with a caressing hand on his starched shirtfront. The sharp scent of Brad's aftershave hit Holly with the force of a dozen memories, helping to shore up her courage.

"I've got more than accounting software on my mind," Holly said, lowering her voice seductively.

Brad lifted her hand from his shirt, then straightened his glasses and peered closely at her. "You should get that hoarseness checked out," he said, stepping backward. "Might be bronchitis."

For a second, Holly wished she did have some virulent, highly contagious illness. Something he could catch from her that would make him feel miserable, but wouldn't be life-threatening.

In her normal voice, she said, "I feel fine. I just think we've been apart long enough, don't you?"

Think sexy, Holly commanded herself. *It's your last chance—be bold.* She advanced toward him and Brad backed up, all the way into his office. Slamming the door shut with her foot—hey, this was fun!—Holly tossed her briefcase onto the leather sofa that lined one wall and reached for her coat sash.

"You didn't really invite me here to look at software, did you, Brad?" she whispered.

"Holly! What's gotten into you?" He was trapped between her and the rosewood executive desk at his back. Brad gaped at her. "This isn't like you at all."

"It's the new me," she murmured, actually starting to enjoy herself. It was like playing a role in a movie. It was like riding a roller coaster, drunk, at midnight. Not that she'd ever really done something like that, but Holly was starting to believe the new, *spontaneous* her just might try it.

Smiling, she finished undoing her coat sash and raised her fingers to the lapels.

"Come home, Brad," she said. "We can be so perfect together; I know we can."

Inch by inch, she slowly opened her coat. His eyes widened. It was just the reaction she'd hoped for. Encouraged, Holly raised her knee to the desk, high enough for Brad to see her garter and the top of her stocking.

The pressure of balancing on one foot snapped the spike heel clean off her shoe. She went down like an anchor tossed overboard.

"Holly! Are you all right?" Brad crouched in front of her and caught hold of her arms. Briefly his gaze dipped to the groping-hands bra, then upward again.

"I'm fine," she said, feeling ridiculous. "Help me up?"

He helped Holly to her feet, then hotfooted it behind his desk, putting some distance between them. While Brad's back was turned, Holly seated herself on the sofa and belted her coat closed again. Somehow, it didn't feel right anymore.

Brad sat down, looking awkward and embarrassed for them both. He stared at his desk blotter, patting the nape of his neck—a sure sign he was mulling something over. Holly crossed her legs, waiting.

"I'm not sure what to make of this," he finally said. "Have you been reading one of those women's magazines or something?"

As a matter of fact, she had. She'd gone to the library and searched the periodicals index for appropriate-looking articles, articles that might spark some ideas for her Plan. Holly wasn't going to admit that to Brad, though.

He straightened in his chair and glanced at her. "This isn't about . . . sex." He cleared his throat, looking vaguely prudish, something she hadn't noticed in Brad before, "It's about making a decision that'll affect my life for years to come. I won't rush into a greater commitment without considering all the factors. It's part of the space thing I've been talking about lately."

Holly leaned back. Okay, so seduction hadn't worked. She was willing to speak practically with him.

"Exactly how long do you think this . . . consideration is going to take?" she asked, slipping off her shoes and setting them atop her briefcase. The motion made the Lover's Potion and Aphrodisia Massage Oil clink together inside. Maybe she could still return the unopened bottles for a full refund. She wasn't likely to find a use for them now.

Brad patted his neck again, then smoothed his open palms over his desk blotter. "I don't know, but I'm very close to making a decision."

Hallelujah. Brad was going to decide their fate.

"I'm not sure how much longer I can wait," Holly said.

It was the end of the line. The end of the Plan. She'd tried everything she could think of, short of handcuffing them together. Even then, Brad would probably resist making a commitment. It had to be up to him now.

"I understand," he said, his forehead wrinkling with concern. "After all, you've probably got that biological ticking clock thing going on. I've been thinking about it. You're not getting any younger, you know."

Holly couldn't believe what she was hearing. "And you're not getting any smarter," she said, rising from the sofa with as much dignity as she could muster.

Gathering her shoes and briefcase, she headed for the office door. There, she stopped. "I need to know what your decision is—about us—by the end of the week."

Brad blinked up at her. After a minute, he asked, "Does this mean you won't evaluate my new accounting software for me?"

Had he always been this self-centered? "I don't know," Holly said, throwing his words back at him, "but I'm very close to making a decision. Bye, Brad."

Chapter Eight

"I've gotta be crazy," Sam said to David mid-morning on Saturday. "Of all the women in this town—"

"And we both know there are so many in Saguaro Vista . . ."

"Of all the women in this town," Sam continued, scowling at Clarissa's husband, "I've got to pick one that's obsessed with another man."

They were sitting on Holly's kitchen floor, trying to pry up the old yellow linoleum so they could lay a new wood floor. It was the last big renovation project to be tackled, but given their progress so far, Sam almost wished they'd chosen something easier—like rewiring the whole house, maybe.

The linoleum seemed to have been welded on somehow. Either that, or the original concrete slab was really an eight-inch-thick slab of linoleum. Sam picked up a heavy metal spatula and pried at the one corner he'd managed to loosen. It barely moved.

"She'll come around," David said. "Holly's a smart girl."

He rammed a spatula beneath the section of linoleum he was working on and pulled. About an inch of flooring came up. David swore.

"Louder. Maybe you can cuss it out of there," Sam told him, grinning.

Of all the men who worked for his dad's construction company, David was the only one who'd agreed to help Sam with Holly's renovation project. As soon as they'd heard the job was renovating Holly Aldridge's house, they'd all found other things to do with their weekends than earn a few extra bucks. Sam didn't understand it.

"I know Holly's smart," Sam said, returning to their earlier conversation. "What I didn't bargain on is how determined she is, too. She doesn't know the meaning of surrender."

David stopped prying at the linoleum long enough to point the spatula toward Sam. "And you do?"

Sam laughed. David had him there. "I'll surrender just as soon as Holly does," he said. "Until then, I'm going to do my damnedest to convince her we belong together."

The slam of the screen door put an end to their conversation. A few seconds later, Holly stomped past the archway into the living room. There was a thud as something hit the floor, then the sound of Holly muttering to herself.

"I don't know, Holly. What's gotten into you, Holly? Might be bronchitis, Holly." Her voice was low-pitched, a pissed-off imitation of a man's voice—Brad's voice, if Sam guessed correctly.

She came into the kitchen, clutching a pair of red high-heeled shoes to her chest, still muttering. She was dressed in a raincoat. Holly dropped the shoes onto the counter and frowned at them. A small red thing rolled off the countertop and landed on the other side, almost in Sam's lap. It was one of her heels.

Sam held it up. "I can fix this for you, if you want," he offered.

Holly screamed.

She lurched over the counter, staring at him.

"Why didn't you say you were down there?" she demanded. "You just about gave me a heart attack."

"I didn't mean to scare you," Sam said, looking back at her. She'd done something to her hair—there was a pouffy spot on top big enough to stash a pack of gum in, and it was all curly on the ends. It looked good, in a wild kind of way.

Holly looked down at the ripped-up floor, then at the two of them sitting amidst their spatulas, the heat gun, assorted tools, and Sam's opened red toolbox. Her gaze rested for a second on the jumbo bag of nacho chips he and David had shared for breakfast, then moved up to Sam again.

"Are you sure you two are doing this right?" she asked doubtfully. "The floor looks worse than ever."

"It's supposed to look this way," David interrupted, saving Sam from answering. "How ya' doing, Holly?"

"Fine, thanks." From the sound of it, she'd rather chew nails than talk civilly to anyone.

"Oookay . . . Sorry I asked." David grinned and went back to work again.

Holly took a deep breath, visibly trying to calm herself. She gave David a wavery, apologetic smile. "I'm sorry, David. You guys want some help? I can change and be back in a couple of minutes . . ."

She touched her fingers to her coat lapels, started pulling them apart, then stopped. Her face reddened. Surprisingly, so did her chest. Sam hadn't realized a woman could blush all the way down to ... down to where her shirt should be, if she was wearing one. Holly wasn't wearing a shirt. Probably, she wasn't wearing much of anything else, either.

Holly shoved the raincoat closed again, holding it tight against her throat.

"I'll be right back," she said, turning toward the archway.

All at once, Sam understood.

"How's Brad these days?" he asked.

Holly stopped, holding onto the archway edges with both hands. Her fingers tightened.

"None of your business," she told him, raising her head. Then, suddenly decisive, she turned back and marched all the way over to the middle of the dining room where he and David were sitting.

"How did you know?"

"It didn't take a genius to figure out all those lingerie bags in the trash. But your raincoat was the dead giveaway."

Sam gazed down at her broken heel, still in his hand. "What I can't figure out is how this happened," he went on, grinning at her. "You want to tell us about it?"

David looked interested. Holly looked mad.

"No." Holly turned, scooped up her shoes from the counter, and headed for the living room.

Sam waved the heel of her shoe. "You want me to fix this, or what?" he called.

He couldn't stop smiling. If Brad could turn down Holly—and he must have—when she was wearing nothing but a raincoat and some sexy lingerie ... well, Sam's chance of a future with her looked a whole lot brighter all of a sudden.

Holly belted her raincoat tighter, then came back and snatched the heel away. "No. I'll fix it myself."

She examined the little nails embedded in the broken heel, flipped over the shoe, and centered the heel in place.

Biting her lip thoughtfully, she glanced around the kitchen, studiously ignoring him. A second later, her eyes lit up. Picking up her other shoe, Holly held it like a hammer, high above her head. She took a deep breath and slammed it down hard onto the broken heel.

The heel flew off like a red leather bullet, straight at Sam's head.

"Ow!"

Distantly, Sam heard the heel clatter to the floor. Holly gasped and skidded across the linoleum to where Sam sat, clutching his head with one hand. It still stung where the heel had smacked into it.

"Oh, Sam—I'm so sorry! Are you okay?"

Gently, she lifted his hand away. "I don't think you're bleeding," she said, peering at his scalp.

Beside him, David picked up the broken heel and held it out to Holly. "Here you—"

"Oh, no you don't!" Sam grabbed it, glaring at them both. "You want to arm her again? I thought you were my friend."

He shook off Holly's hand and got up. Taking the heel from David, Sam picked up the broken shoe from the counter.

"*I'll* fix this," he said, giving them both a look that dared them to disagree. He shouldn't have been surprised when Holly did. She grabbed for the broken shoe.

Sam held it just out of reach. She gave a little jump; he lifted it higher.

"I can fix it," she told him. "I've gotten along just fine until now without your stupid he-man fix-it routine, you know. I'm not helpless."

He-man? "You're a menace," he shot back.

"Give me my shoe, please." The words emerged through clenched teeth, just before Holly jumped again.

She missed, probably because Sam was about half a foot taller than she was. It wasn't difficult to keep the shoe away from her.

Sam had a devious thought.

"Show me what's under your coat," he offered, "and I'll give you your shoe back."

"What? No."

"Come on," Sam coaxed, dangling her shoe—the bait—just out of reach. He grinned.

She kicked him in the shin.

"Ow!" He dropped her shoe. Holly picked it up with a smug little smile and flounced off, muttering something about getting into some normal clothes for a change, so she could help.

Sam stopped her. "Oh, no—you're not helping."

"What? Why not?"

"We've already covered this ground, haven't we?"

She glared at him.

"You're not going to kick me again, are you?"

Holly shook her head. "Come on, Sam. I'm having kind of a hard day. Why don't you quit trying to change the subject and just tell me why you don't want me to help?"

"Because you're dangerous, that's why."

Looking offended, Holly crossed her arms over her chest. "Only when provoked," she said. "I asked you nicely to give me my shoe, and you didn't."

She nodded at the broken heel. "Hitting you with that was an accident, and you know it."

"So was breaking my toe with that damned ten-pound book," Sam pointed out, waggling his bare foot. So what if it was already healed? "Now you want me to let you wreak havoc on the floor? With tools?" He shook his head. "I'd have to be crazy."

David grinned at that. "What was that you were saying earlier about being crazy?"

Sam cut him off with a look. He didn't need to be reminded how he'd called himself crazy, and crazy about Holly, just fifteen minutes ago. David shrugged and dug into the bag of nacho chips at his feet, removing himself from the argument.

"It's my floor," Holly insisted. "I want to help. All you have to do is show me how." She glanced down at the shards of yellow linoleum scattered at their feet. "It doesn't look too difficult to me."

She gave him a shrewd look. "Maybe you don't want me to find out how easy this is. It would hurt your handyman's ego."

Her gaze darted over to David. "Is that why he won't let me help?"

David looked about to choke on a nacho chip with the effort of holding back a laugh.

"Well," he said, glancing speculatively at Sam. "I dunno—you worried about your masculine ego, Sam?"

If the nacho chip didn't get him, Sam promised himself he'd do the job later.

He frowned at Holly. "You really believe that?"

"No," she replied, "but I really do want to help. I've been working all week and I haven't had a chance to do anything. Come on, Sam. I'm a quick study, you'll see."

She smiled encouragingly. Sam decided to surrender to the inevitable before she dug any deeper. "Fine. Have it your way."

Her smile deepened. Sam's didn't. He felt like a sap. Holly turned and headed for the bedroom to change clothes. Too bad he couldn't persuade her to keep the raincoat and lingerie on.

"Be sure to put on something old," Sam warned. "Whatever you wear's going to get wrecked."

She waved a hand over her head. "Okay, I'll be right back!"

Sam looked over at David.

"We're in for it now," he grumbled.

He was more right than he'd expected, but not in the way he'd thought. A few minutes later when Holly emerged from the bedroom, Sam stopped in mid-scrape to stare. Holly's wild new hairstyle was small change compared to how she looked geared up for renovating.

"These are the oldest, grungiest things I could find," she said, waving her hand at her faded University of Arizona T-shirt and old denim cutoff shorts. "Okay?"

"Uh, okay." Sam tried to quit staring, but it was impossible. In those shorts, Holly looked completely different. It was a glimpse of the kind of woman she must've been before Brad and his tight-assed ways got hold of her, before she'd plotted out her plan for life and set the map in stone. He wondered if it was too late to smash the map apart and start over again.

But that would have to come later. For now he'd have to settle for teaching Holly how to tear up an old linoleum floor. Kneeling next to her, Sam showed her how to look at the edges of the floor for places that had lifted up over the years, then pry them up further with a heavy metal spatula. He showed her how to pour in a little adhesive solvent beneath to loosen the glue, and how to scrape up the stubborn pieces that sometimes remained, so the subfloor would be level.

When Sam turned around to check on her progress a few minutes later, Holly was working diligently. Beside her was the evidence of her labor—a tidy stack of linoleum pieces, a dustpan filled with debris, and the nacho chip bag, now filled with linoleum shards. For a radius of two feet around her, the floor was swept conspicuously clean.

Holly was on her hands and knees, mopping it with a sponge.

"We're not going to eat from this floor," Sam said, trying to keep his grin hidden. "Work first, clean later."

She didn't stop.

"A neat workspace will make the job go quicker," she replied, a little breathless from her enthusiastic mopping. Next Holly whipped out an old towel and dried the floor, her backside swinging enticingly in rhythm with each stroke of the towel.

Her denim cutoffs revealed more than they hid, especially in the places where she'd dried her damp hands on them. Beneath the soft, thin fabric of her old T-shirt, her breasts kept time, too, swaying gently as she worked. Sam's gut tightened. He really was crazy.

Clapping his hands together to dislodge the worst of the dirt, Sam looked at David and Holly in turn. "What do you say we break for lunch?"

When they didn't answer, he raised his eyebrows. "Lunch?"

"Well, I'm still pretty full," David said, glancing at the nacho chip bag.

Sam scowled and got to his feet. "Then you can stay here and finish up while Holly and I go to lunch," he said. He turned to her. "Do you want to change first?"

She looked exasperated. "I just did, remember? What's wrong with what I've got on?"

"Nothing." Nothing except that it made Sam want to take all of it off. Nothing except that it showed him a side to Holly he'd never seen before, and he liked it—too much.

"Nothing," Sam said again, "I just thought you'd want to wear something more . . . ah,"—he searched his brain for a reason that would appeal to her—"something more appropriate."

Something *un*sexy.

"You sound just like Brad," Holly accused, scrambling to stand up on the slippery linoleum. She pointed a finger in Sam's face. "Well, I'm through with men telling me what to do and what to wear and who to see, do you hear me?"

Sam backed up, pushed more by the impact of her unexpected temper than the long pink fingernail she was poking at him. He'd obviously touched a nerve, telling her to look appropriate. It wasn't a mistake he wanted to repeat in the future.

"I'll do what I want, when I want to do it," Holly went on, her voice rising. "If I want to dance naked on *my* floor, in *my* kitchen, in *my* house, then I'll do it! And you can't stop me!"

"Why would he want to?" David put in, grinning. Holly threw her wet sponge at him. It landed with a wet splat on his nose, then plopped to the floor.

She was spoiling for a fight. She looked at Sam as though she were mentally rolling up her sleeves, a prizefighter ready for the next match.

Sam held up both hands in surrender. "Okay! Wear what you want."

"I will," Holly said, flouncing away. So much for his brilliant plan to get her into some different clothes. Maybe next time he ought to try reverse psychology. For now he'd have to admit defeat. Maybe if they went some place dark ... hell, he was a grown man, wasn't he? It would take more than the sight of Holly in a pair of short shorts, looking fresh from a roll in the hay, to take Sam McKenzie down.

In the foyer, Holly paused, keys in hand. "You fellas coming, or not?"

Sam nodded.

"We'll take my car," she announced when he and David got to the front door. She looked about six inches taller, flush with the thrill of running the show. Proud of herself. And despite everything, Sam was glad for her. Maybe that road map of hers was splintering a little already.

Holly could've kicked herself for saying they'd take her car. She'd been so pleased with the way she'd asserted herself with Sam, she'd forgotten there were three of them going to lunch—one more than would fit comfortably into her two-seater convertible.

To their credit, neither Sam nor David said a thing about her mistake as they piled into Sam's old pickup truck instead. Sam got behind the wheel, and Holly slid across the wide bench seat to take her place in the middle, leaving David smashed up against the passenger-side door. To give him more room, Holly scooted a little closer to Sam.

The truck was just like Sam—big, messy, but in perfect running order. When he turned the ignition key, the engine purred to life as quietly as a luxury sportscar's, and the stereo system Sam turned on sounded even better than the expensive one Brad had so rudely repossessed after their split.

Sam raised his eyebrows, seeking her approval of the radio station he'd tuned, and Holly nodded, surprised he'd bother to check with her at all. She probably shouldn't have been. From the day she'd met him, Sam had wanted to please her. To pleasure her. In that, too, he was exactly *un*like Brad. She shivered and turned her attention to the things jumbled inside the truck, a much safer subject than Sam's feelings for her.

Her inspection ended abruptly with the warm, unexpected feeling of Sam's hand on her bare thigh. Her gaze shot downward. His hand slid further along the inside of her thigh, moving down toward her knee until his tanned arm lay against her, then he gripped . . . the gearshift. It was right between her legs.

Their eyes met.

"Excuse me," Sam said. "Hope this won't be too uncomfortable for you."

The sparkle in his eyes told her he wasn't *too* sorry about their driving arrangement. Trying to retain the upper hand, Holly shrugged.

"As long as you're not uncomfortable," she said solicitously, "I guess I can stand it as long as you can."

His thumb stroked her thigh. "I'll remember that," Sam promised with a wink, then he set the truck into motion.

Sam could make a grocery list read like erotic innuendo, Holly thought. She didn't know how he managed it. *Maybe you want it to sound that way,* a part of her nudged. *Maybe you're the one who wants* him.

She shoved the thought aside and tried to focus on the scenery as Sam drove into town. She tried not to think about the hungry way Sam had looked at her this morning, when he'd realized how little she had on beneath her trench coat. She tried not to remember the feel of Sam's body against hers, tried not to relive the kisses they'd shared, tried not to reexperience the heat and intensity of his mouth on hers.

Who was she kidding?

Holly sighed. Being around Sam made her priorities go so far underground she couldn't remember what she wanted anymore. She remembered feeling certain that Brad was the right man for her, that marrying him was the only sensible thing to do. She'd thought he was the ideal man to share the future with.

All of a sudden, that future looked awfully bleak.

She didn't want to fail. That's what it would be, if her Plan didn't bring her and Brad back together again. Failure. She'd probably ensured it by giving Brad a deadline to decide about their future together. Holly hadn't been able to think of another alternative. She didn't want to end up like her mother had after the divorce—alone. Alone and . . . yes, a little bitter, too. Holly supposed that a great, passionate love gone wrong could do that to anybody.

Even Sam? She glanced over at him. As usual, he was wearing old faded jeans and an attitude so relaxed that being with him was like the best vacation she'd ever had. As though he sensed her gaze on him, he gave her a smile and then looked back at the road. No, Holly decided, probably not Sam. Love wouldn't dare go wrong on Sam.

They had lunch at the Downtown Grill, and afterward dropped David off at Holly's to pick up his car. Still sitting in the driveway in Sam's truck, they watched him make a U-turn in the street and then drive away.

"So, should we go in and finish up the linoleum?" Sam asked. He looked like he'd rather dye his hair green than go back inside and scrape more linoleum.

"No, I've got other plans for you."

"Really?" He nudged closer and wrapped his arm around her shoulders. "Tell me all about it."

"Well,"—Holly smiled up at him, feeling better now that she'd been fortified with a double cheeseburger and fries—"first we'll go to the formal wear shop downtown . . ."

"Yeah . . . ?"

"And then we'll pick up your tuxedo. Did you forget my mother's party at the Cheshire is tonight?"

Sam groaned and started the engine. "I thought you were kidding about wearing a tuxedo."

"Nope. I already ordered one for you, just in case you, ahh . . . forgot." Her smile broadened.

"You don't leave much to chance, do you?"
"Not usually. Let's go."

At the formal wear shop, Holly picked up the dress she'd ordered for the party, and Sam reluctantly accepted a black tuxedo and the full dress regalia that went along with it.

"Just to make sure the dress fits before I take it home, can I try it on, please?" Holly asked the salesperson.

"Certainly," the gray-haired woman replied, nodding toward a curtained area at the rear of the small shop. "Right through there."

"Thanks." Holly headed toward the changing rooms, chose one of the three mirrored alcoves, and pulled the curtain closed behind her. She hung her dress on the hook provided and quickly shucked her shorts and T-shirt. Brad had always hated shopping with her, and Holly supposed most men were the same way—including Sam. She wanted to hurry so he wouldn't have long to wait.

Someone entered the cubicle next to hers and dragged the curtain shut with the metallic scrape of the hanging rings against the chrome rod. Whoever it was, she was tall—Holly glimpsed a headful of shaggy blond hair over the partition before she bent down again. Holly shrugged and stepped into her new dress. She zipped it up, arranged the shoulder straps, and looked into the mirror.

It was a great dress, the sexiest-looking one she'd ever owned. White, mid-thigh length, and close-fitting, it needed only a matching sheer chiffon scarf to accessorize it. Holly arranged the scarf casually over her throat, leaving the ends to trail down the low-cut dress back, and scrutinized the effect.

"You look great in white," said Sam's voice. "It sets off all that red hair of yours."

He winked down at her from the neighboring dressing room. Holly decided the expensive designer dress was worth every single cent it was costing her.

"You're not supposed to be back here. What are you doing?" she whispered.

Sam propped his arms atop the partition, making it wobble a little. "Trying on my stuff," he answered reasonably. "There are only these three little rooms, you know. Was I supposed to change out there in front of the three-way mirror like one of those Chippendale's guys?"

Holly pictured him doing an exotic-dancer's bump and grind routine, slowly stripping off his clothes in front of the big mirror. The idea had merit.

"Of course not." The way he was looking at her, she couldn't resist preening a little in her new dress. Pivoting, Holly looked over her shoulder at him. "Do you really like it?"

"Come next door and I'll show you how much."

"I'm serious."

"So am I." Sam grinned and disappeared from sight behind the partition. There was a rustle of fabric, then the sound of a zipper, and he reappeared. "Pants fit."

He must've been talking to her in his underwear. "Good," Holly said.

He struggled into the sleeves of his white dress shirt. "I meant what I said," Sam told her. "You look great. The only way you could possibly look better is if you were wearing that white dress at our wedding."

He ducked behind the partition again, swore, and reemerged a minute later with the bow tie draped loosely around his open shirt collar. He waggled one end of it. "Can you help me with this thing? I think it's possessed."

Holly gaped at him. Sam took one look at what had to be her stupefied expression and said, "Never mind. I guess the saleslady can tie it for me. I just won't take off the monkey suit until after the party."

"Did you say, 'our wedding'?"

His expression turned serious. "Yeah. What did you think I had in mind, seducing you and then skipping town the next day?"

He was waiting for her answer, but Holly's brain had somehow turned to Jell-O. She realized that was exactly what she'd thought, that if she let herself fall for Sam it would only mean heartache when he left again.

She nodded, slowly. "Umm, yes." This was getting way too serious. Holly turned toward the mirror again and fiddled with her dress strap, trying to disguise her confusion.

"Aren't all men commitment-phobic, anyway?" she asked lightly. "What makes you so different?"

The curtain slid away and Sam was there. He closed it behind him, secluding them both in the tiny cubicle. He looked good in a tuxedo, even with it only half-on. No, make that, especially with it only half-on. Holly had a brief, ridiculous impulse to duck beneath his outstretched arms and run as far away as she could. It didn't happen because she couldn't move.

"I'm different because I'm the man who loves you."

"You shouldn't be in here, and you shouldn't say things like that, either, and not so loud," Holly babbled. "Somebody might hear you."

"I don't care who hears me." Sam moved closer and his hands slipped between her arms and chest to pull her to him.

"I'll take out a billboard if it means you'll listen. I'll put an ad in the paper." He grinned. "I'll wear one of those signs you strap on and walk around with. I'm in love with you."

"You—you only think that," Holly said, looking up at the walls, the curtain, down at her feet—any place but at him. Why had they started talking about this in the first place? Hadn't she had enough cold reality for one day?

His fingers splayed along her shoulder blades, lightly teasing her bare skin. Halfheartedly, she tried to shrug them away. "It's only that love-at-first-sight thing."

"Not anymore."

Sam drew her closer, his fingertips pressing harder. When his mouth lowered to hers, Holly stopped thinking altogether. The kiss was slow and deliberate and filled with passion, sweetened by longing. It was a kiss that hinted of promise and possessiveness, and when it was over she was limp in Sam's arms.

Just when she thought he must be getting tired of holding her up in the cramped cubicle, Sam looked down at her and asked, "Is that proof enough for you?"

Holly blinked at him and rational thought returned.

"No. It only proves there's a ... a sexual attraction between us," she said, putting a good eight inches between them by retreating to the tiny triangular bench in the changing room corner. She felt damp, and disheveled, and fiercely aroused.

"Nothing more," Holly insisted. "You've got that love-at-first-sight thing in your head, and you're too stubborn to give it up."

"I'm not the only stubborn one," Sam pointed out. "Are you saying all this to convince me—or to convince yourself?"

With a sigh, Holly pressed her thighs together to stop the ache he'd aroused—just a natural reaction, she assured herself—and glanced up at him. Sam leaned a shoulder against the partition and stuffed both hands in his pockets. He didn't say anything else.

"You have a life in another city, a life I know almost nothing about, aside from the bare facts," Holly said. "And I—"

"What do you want to know?"

"Oh, Sam, that's not the point. Don't you see?" She felt like crying, caught between hope and fear and a bunch of feelings she'd never experienced before. At least there was logical thought to cling to. "You have your life, and I have mine, and they're happening in different places. When the summer's over with, you'll go back."

Sam was shaking his head, but she couldn't stop until he understood.

"You drop the idea of marriage on me like it's as easy as picking what brand of toothpaste to buy. I'll bet you haven't thought, really *thought*, about any of this."

"I spend most of my time thinking of you."

But that wasn't the same as planning a future together. Holly shook her head. He didn't understand, and she didn't know how else to explain it. But she couldn't resist when Sam dropped to his knees in front of her and wrapped his arms around her, resting his head on the tops of her thighs. His hair was silky against her bare skin. She felt him breathe deeply, then he hugged her tighter.

"It'll work out," Sam said, his voice muffled. "We can make all those details work, Holly."

Her throat tightened. She wanted to believe it, wanted to believe him. She wanted to be as sure as Sam was. But she couldn't.

"How?" she whispered. "What about my job—and yours? Where would we live? Oh, Sam—how can it work out?"

He was silent. Tentatively, she raised a hand to Sam's head and buried her fingers in his hair, stroking. It felt good. *He* felt good—and so did Holly, when she was with him. But was it enough?

"Ms. Aldridge, are you all right?" The voice came from outside the dressing room, but it was growing louder. "Mr. McKenzie, where are you?"

The salesperson pulled open the curtain. It only took one look at Sam's head buried in Holly's lap to get both of them kicked out of the formal wear shop—for life.

Chapter Nine

The Cheshire Hotel was the finest in all of Saguaro Vista. It catered as much to the golfing crowd that spilled over from the city golf course as it did to the temporarily-resident senior citizens who liked to spend their winters someplace warmer than Minnesota.

In mid-June, though, the Cheshire was filled with locals, the kind of people who thought a ninety-five-degree day almost called for a jacket. As she and Sam stepped into the frigid, air-conditioned lobby, Holly agreed with them.

"Thanks for bringing me," she said, looking up at him.

Making a face, she confessed, "Big formal parties aren't really my thing. I'd hate to face this alone."

Sam smiled at her. "You're not alone anymore."

His words had such a wonderful sound. Even when she'd planned her life with Brad, Holly hadn't thought of them as being truly together, two halves of one whole. Their lives had already been more separate than that, she realized. If Brad's decision was to move their relationship forward, she'd have to find a way to deal with that.

They headed toward the room where her mother's party was in progress.

Thinking of the incident in the formal wear shop, Holly said, "Once word gets around about this afternoon, I'll probably *never* be alone. The owner is one of the biggest gossips around—people probably think I'm the town hussy by now."

For some reason, the idea of being on the receiving end of the townspeople's censure didn't bother her as much as it used to. Holly knew she'd done nothing wrong, and that seemed more important.

She grinned up at Sam. "They'll be lining up to date me," she joked. "You'll see."

His arm tightened around her waist. "Not if I have anything to say about it."

At the party, Holly's mother was the first to greet them. She floated over, doubtless fueled by several martinis, and linked arms with her daughter.

"I'm so glad you both could come," Linda said, smiling.

Amazingly, her smile seemed genuine. Even Holly, who'd been expecting disapproval instead, was convinced. It was a relief to know her mother wouldn't disown her for appearing in public without Brad.

"Thanks, Mom." Holly nudged Sam. "Doesn't my date look handsome?"

Linda looked Sam up and down, from the top of his head to the soles of his dress shoes, and said, "Yes, he does. You clean up nicely, Stan."

"Sam."

"Oh, of course. I'm sorry." She turned to Holly and

frowned. "But you didn't try that hairdresser I told you about, did you?" Licking a fingertip, she carefully swept her daughter's hair away from her face. "No, I can see you didn't—your hair still has that *rumpled* look, dear."

"I like it this way, Mom," Holly said, but she gritted her teeth and dutifully endured her mother's fussing. When Linda was finished, she stepped back to survey her handiwork.

"There," she said, looking satisfied. Holly stifled the urge to pull her hair back down over her ears and smiled back at her. "Now I've got to go speak with Mayor Anderson about his new house, so if you'll both excuse me?"

They said their goodbyes, and Linda disappeared into the crowd of brightly dressed women and tuxedo-clad men. Holly watched her go with a clear sense of relief. After having all but refused to go to the party unless Sam escorted her, she'd been worried about how her mother would react. It looked as though the only problem her mother had with Sam, though, was remembering his name.

"You know," Sam said after Linda had gone, "your mother has an overdeveloped mothering instinct. But I think she means well."

Surprised, Holly looked up at him. "You do?"

"Sure. If she didn't care, she wouldn't spend all that energy trying to tell you what was best for you."

Grinning, Sam accepted two margaritas from a passing waiter and handed one to Holly. "To true love," he said, raising his glass.

"And to relentless men," Holly said, raising hers also.

"Touché."

They both drank. Sam set his glass down on a damask-skirted table, looked around, and asked, "Now that we've greeted, made an appearance, and toasted each other, can we slip out of this shindig?"

"You don't like parties either?"

Sam made a face, tugging at his bow tie. "Not this kind. I've had enough of these press-the-flesh, networking things to last a lifetime. But I'll stay if you want to."

Holly thought about it. "Now that she's already talked

to us and restyled my hair, I don't think my mother will miss us if we make an early getaway. There are just a few people I want to say hello to."

Her "few people" took nearly an hour to say hello to, especially since she had to introduce Sam to each one. Surprisingly, no one asked her about Brad, and for that Holly was grateful. She didn't want to make any explanations, at least until everything was settled between them.

Afterward, she and Sam walked together toward the terrace exit, then stepped onto the saltillo tile that led outside. A row of luminarias, filled with clean sand and lighted candles, lined each side of the path around the hotel's exterior, making it a nice spot for an evening walk. Sam caught hold of her hand and squeezed gently.

"Why do you have to go to so many parties, if you don't like them?" Holly asked him, reaching up to brush her fingertips along the canopy of feathery mesquite tree leaves overhead.

"Goes with the job," he said, shrugging. "I guess there's a certain amount of glad-handing that goes with any kind of work."

"But construction?"

"No, my other job—my faraway life in Tucson, remember? The road to tenure is paved with hard work, publication, and about a million faculty parties."

Sam looked so aggrieved at that, Holly had to laugh. "See, that's exactly what I was talking about earlier. I've spent so much time seeing you rip my house apart—"

"Hey, I think the remodeling is going well!"

"—That I forget about your alter-ego, the college professor. What's it like?"

They passed an open archway, and the sounds of music and conversation drifted outside. A minute later the sounds of revelry were muted again, replaced by the night song of cicadas.

"It's probably not like you imagine it," Sam replied. "Less ivy-covered halls of academia and more *Animal House*. I teach night classes—Composition, and Literature, and some remedial English—mostly to returning students."

"Dropouts?"

His expression was indecipherable. "Sometimes. Or just people who've had life interfere once too often with their plans. They're the ones old enough,"—he frowned—"no, determined enough—to really value what they're learning."

He pulled her close, turning Holly in his arms. "And that's probably more than you ever wanted to know about any of it," he said, and with no warning at all, Sam danced her the rest of the way down the luminaria-lit path.

She was breathless by the time they stopped at the edge of the hotel parking lot. So was Sam, but he didn't seem to mind. Holly decided she should've been taking spontaneity lessons from Sam all along. He made it seem effortless.

"What do you say we head for the lake?" he asked her. "I've got a sudden yen for a swim."

"At this hour? It's dark out. Besides, we'd have to go home first and get swimsuits," Holly argued.

"Who said anything about swimsuits?"

She put both hands on her hips. "Well, I'm not ruining my new dress just because you feel like taking a dip in the lake."

Sam winked. "Who said anything about wearing clothes?"

Forty-five minutes and half as many miles later, Sam was naked as the day he was born, chest-deep in the warm water of Lake Pleasant. It had been his summer hangout as a teenager; now, years later, things hadn't changed much. The water was still pretty shallow for a good half-block in, and the lake bottom was still rocky enough to require a pair of shoes if you didn't want to risk bruising the soles of your feet.

Sam ducked his head underwater, and came up shaking drops of it from his hair. "Come on in, the water's fine," he called to Holly.

She shook her head and held her ground at the water's edge. He couldn't read her expression, but the moonlight caught every sexy curve beneath her white dress, teasing him with her nearness. So close and yet so far.

"Don't make me come over there and get you," he warned with a grin.

She didn't budge. Sam took a deep breath and swam toward the shore.

"You wouldn't dare," Holly said when he was halfway there.

"I wouldn't?"

He stood up, making rivulets of water run from his body down into the lake again. Holly developed a sudden, apparently overwhelming interest in the distant rocky cliffs that lined the lake's edge. She crossed her arms over her chest, staring fixedly into the distance. On a flat rock just behind her, his dress shoes, tuxedo, and shirt lay where he'd dropped them—now folded neatly, thanks to Holly.

"Nobody can see us." Sam started towards her through the shallows, goose bumps prickling his skin. It was a lot warmer in the water than out of it.

"I never said I'd go skinny-dipping with you," Holly reminded him, digging her big toe in the sand. She'd taken off her shoes and, while his back was turned, her stockings. Both were safely stowed on the rock beside his clothes.

Holly chewed her lip, looking vaguely guilty. "I'm not . . . well, you might as well know. I'm not really the spontaneous type. It was all an act."

"You're kidding."

"It's true. I can't help it." Sam came closer, and she backed up. "I even planned the whole spontaneity thing."

"If you're trying to scare me off, it won't work. I'm already hooked." He smiled. "I'm at your mercy."

Her eyebrows lifted and Holly did look at him then, but only at his face. "You're at my mercy?"

"Absolutely."

He was almost close enough to grab her, almost close enough to drip lake water onto her bare feet. Sam was laying himself bare for her, naked in every way. The idea of that was enough to send a sane man screaming to the hills, but he wanted Holly to know the man who loved her. If that made him crazy, then Sam didn't care.

"Okay, then," Holly said, narrowing her eyes at him in a contemplative, amused look. "If you're really at my mercy, prove it."

"What do you want me to do?"

"Stand back. I'm afraid you're going to toss me into the water."

Sam laughed. "Very perceptive. The idea had crossed my mind."

"Well?"

"Anything but that." He scooped her into his arms and carried her toward the water.

"Let me go!"

"If you don't quit kicking and wriggling, I might just drop you." Sam stopped at the water's edge and looked down at the woman in his arms, then grinned. "Well?"

"Okay, okay," Holly relented. "Just let me down so I don't ruin my dress in the water."

"Deal."

As soon as her feet touched the sand, she was off running. Her white dress flashing, Holly sped to the flat rock, snatched all his clothes, then ran away down the beach. Her feet pounded against the hard-packed sand, gaining speed with every step. That was Holly—making him chase her for every little inch of progress.

Sam chased her across the moonlit beach, around a cove where she made a U-turn back toward their starting point, and partway back before he caught up to her. Reaching out both arms, he pulled her back against him and held her tight. She was laughing.

"You're pretty fast," he said, panting a little.

Holly stood a little straighter. "I do work out at the gym, you know," she informed him between breaths. She held his clothes in a death grip against her chest. "If I'd had a little more of a head start, I'll bet you wouldn't have caught me at all."

"I would've caught you." Digging one hand into her hair, Sam tipped her head back and kissed her, hard.

She welcomed him with a ferocity that matched his own. God, he wanted her. He dragged Holly closer, loving the feel of her tight against him, the feel of her breasts pressed into his bare chest. Dimly, Sam realized she must've dropped his clothes someplace. He didn't care.

They fell to their knees in the sand, mouths still exploring, and all he wanted was to never stop touching her. Gently he tugged the gauzy scarf from her neck and kissed her there, too—small, deliberate bites, then tongue-sweet kisses along the base of her throat. Holly moaned, and the low, husky sounds she made were potent as wine. They sent desire shivering through him. She felt it, too, felt and breathed desire with every sigh, savored it with every bite of her fingernails against his back.

"Oh, Sam . . ."

It was too much and not enough, all at once. Sam cupped her breasts, and her nipples rose to meet his thumbs. He stroked slowly, slower, making the good feelings last. Holly made him feel something beyond simple desire, beyond anything he'd experienced before. He wanted to strip away her dress, wanted to take her there on the sand. He wanted somebody to shut off the lights that were shining into his eyes.

Sam looked up, past Holly. There was a jeep parked about fifty feet away. Its headlights and roll bar lights were trained directly on them. Beyond the brightness, he saw the silhouetted figure of a uniformed, pot-bellied man.

"Break it up, folks," he drawled. "This here's a private beach, and it's closed for the night."

The state trooper—Sam realized that had to be who it was, judging by the uniform—motioned with his flashlight.

"I'd hate to have to arrest you both for indecent exposure, too, along with the trespassing charge," he said without a trace of regret. "So you'd best put your clothes on, sonny."

SURRENDER

* * *

"I can't believe he actually arrested us."

Shaking her head, Holly gripped the cold bars of the holding cell that the highway patrol officer had put her and Sam into at the county jail. She peered down the dank corridor leading to the front of the jail. No action there. Except for the snoring of the drunk who'd been asleep in the adjacent cell when they arrived, everything was quiet.

Behind her, one of the gray metal cots squeaked as Sam sat on it. He rested his forearms on his thighs and loosely clasped his hands together, looking almost as relaxed as he had in the middle of Lake Pleasant. He was dressed now, except for his tuxedo jacket and tie. They lay where he'd tossed them at the foot of the cot's mattress.

"I feel like a criminal," Holly complained, brushing vainly at the beach sand clinging to her new dress. The matching scarf was gone—probably floating in the lake. She ran her tongue over her teeth, wishing fervently for a toothbrush.

She headed for the cot—barefoot, because they'd kept her high-heels for some inexplicable reason—and stopped in front of Sam. There was no way she'd actually sit on the mattress. Who knew what kind of people had used that thing?

"But then I guess I have a criminal record now, don't I?" Holly went on. "I've been arrested and booked into jail."

Booked into jail. "Booked into" sounded wrong, like she'd made reservations at an exclusive resort. Sure—*Casa de la Criminal.*

None of this seemed to be making a dent with Sam. Holly waved her arms wildly at him. "Into jail!" she wailed, feeling slightly hysterical. "Do you know I've never even been *inside* a place like this before, much less been thrown into one?"

She paced across the gritty concrete floor. "Here I am, in jail," she muttered, halfway to herself. "The slammer, the joint, the hoosegow—dear Lord, what am I *doing* here?"

Sam looked calmly back at her. "It's only a trespassing charge," he said. "The most we'll get is a night in jail and a fine, and that's only if the property owner decides to press charges."

Holly gaped at him. "What are you, a career criminal?"

"I've had my share of scrapes with the law."

"What?"

This was what she got for being spontaneous. She'd become involved with a wanted man. A felon—an ex-con, maybe. It sounded like a bad late-night B movie. *Babes Behind Bars, Part Two—Sam Returns.* Holly grabbed the cell bars again and gazed toward the door leading to freedom. She might have known changing her life would lead to disaster.

"It wasn't anything serious," Sam said. "Some stupid high school pranks, a couple of drunk-and-disorderly charges—I've changed my ways since then."

He tried a grin. Holly wasn't having it. Sure he was charming—the dangerous ones always were, weren't they?

"I'll just bet you've changed your ways! Changed them right into jail again, you mean. Why didn't you tell me you'd been arrested before?"

"It never came up." Sam shrugged. "This thing will blow over in no time, you'll see. Don't worry. Everything will be fine."

"Fine? No, it won't be fine."

She felt like shrieking at him, but she didn't. Holly was afraid they'd put her and Sam in separate cells if they argued too loudly. The only thing worse than being locked up in a jail cell would be being locked up in a jail cell without Sam.

She was still mad, though—mad and scared. Holly jabbed her forefinger at Sam's chest.

"This is what comes of being irresponsible," she told him. "This is what comes of crazy stunts like skinny-dipping in the lake at midnight. This—" she paused for emphasis "—is what happens when you don't plan ahead."

Her point made, Holly stomped to the other end of their cell and crossed her arms over her chest, not looking at him. Wait until the people at her office heard about this—she'd probably be fired on the spot. And after all her hard work, too. It just wasn't fair. Why, oh why, had she let Sam talk her into going to the lake with him?

"You can't plan your whole life." He crossed the cell, then stopped behind her. His hands lowered to her shoulders, warm against her bare skin. "You can't plan who you fall in love with." He kissed her shoulder. "Life happens to you. You have to take the good with the bad."

Holly whirled to face him. "Oh, no I don't—I'm not standing by waiting for life to take its chances with me. Only a fool does that. Everything I've gotten, I've gotten because I worked my tail off for it, and I've done a damned good job of it, too!"

Her eyes filled with tears. Why did that always have to happen when she got mad? Angrily, Holly blinked them away.

"So don't you tell me to just take what life hands me," she cried. "Because I won't do it."

"So now I'm a fool, then?" Sam stepped back. "Now I'm the stupid one, because I'm not a compulsive, retentive, Felix Unger wannabe with a retirement plan and a set of matching towels?"

She gasped. "I should never have told you about that!"

"About which, the retirement plan or the towels?"

"Neither!"

"You tell 'em, sister!" shouted the drunk from the next cell. He'd awakened during their argument, and now had his grizzled old face pushed halfway through the bars to watch the final round. He waved his fist in encouragement, then winked at Holly.

"Give 'em what for, honey" he slurred.

Sam's eyes narrowed, and his face darkened. Holly had never seen him mad before; it was an education. Their whole relationship was an education in mistakes not to repeat again.

"Friend of yours?" Sam asked, nodding toward the drunk.

Holly glared at him.

"No, wait—you wouldn't have anything to do with someone who wasn't *perfect*, would you?" he said. "You can't be bothered with somebody who's made a few mistakes."

"Somebody such as . . . an ex-felon like yourself?" Holly inquired with a lift of her eyebrows. "I know better now."

Hurting too much to look at him any longer, she turned away. Sam didn't try to stop her. Stony silence descended upon their cell, only to be broken by the scrape of a key in the door at the end of the corridor. They both looked expectantly toward it.

Brad walked in, followed by the key-wielding guard.

"Somebody page me?" he asked with a grin.

Holly could've cried with relief. Reaching their cell, Brad put his fingers through the bars to clasp her hand. He looked like freshly shaved and showered heaven, right down to the pressed crease in his casual cotton pants. Brad wouldn't have let her down. He'd never have gotten her locked into jail.

"Oh, Brad—thank God you're here," she said, with a meaningful backward glance at Sam's stony face. "It's been awful."

"What the hell is he doing here?" Sam asked.

"He's here to get me out of this godforsaken place. I used my phone call to page him." Brad smiled at her. "Because I *knew* he'd come."

The guard unlocked their cell and swung the barred door open. Brad rushed in and grabbed both her hands. "Are you all right?"

"I . . . I'll be fine," Holly answered. "Once I'm out of this place." *And once I get over Sam.*

"I already called David and Clarissa to bail us out," Sam gritted out through clenched teeth. "They'll be here any minute."

Holly linked arms with her rescuer, then glanced over at Sam. "How was I supposed to know you had a plan to get us out of here?" she asked. "It's not like you've ever planned anything before."

His eyes turned gray with pain. "You're right," Sam said slowly. "If I had, I'd have planned not to fall in love with you."

He held her gaze, daring her to look away first. Daring her to say he didn't really love her.

Holly couldn't do it.

"Goodbye, Sam," she whispered, her throat thick with unshed tears. "I'm sorry things had to end this way."

Chapter Ten

Watching Holly walk away on another man's arm was one of the hardest things Sam had ever had to do. He could only stand, frozen, as she and Brad stepped out of the jail cell and walked together down the corridor. The guard slammed the door shut, locking him in again. Without a backward glance, Holly was gone.

She'd made her choice. Brad.

He should've known better. He should've known a woman like Holly wouldn't really change. She'd told him all along, hadn't she? *I'm trying to work things out with Brad . . . I haven't given up on him yet.*

Not ten minutes later she'd been kissing Sam, responding to him as though they were the hottest of lovers, reunited. So what did that prove? Not a damn thing. Only that they were two healthy, sexual adults who knew a great kiss when they felt one.

Sam dropped onto the narrow cot and lay on his back, one arm thrown over his eyes. He closed them, trying to blot out her image. He shouldn't still want a woman who'd just dumped him. He still wanted Holly. He was an idiot.

The door at the end of the corridor opened again. Sam sat up. Clarissa hurried inside, followed closely by David. She reached his cell and wrapped her fingers around the bars.

"God, Sam—it's been years since I've seen you like this."

Sam grinned, gathering up his jacket and then stuffing his black tie in the pocket. "I'll bet I wasn't wearing a tuxedo last time."

"You look very nice." His cousin wasn't smiling. "Unlock this," she snapped to the guard.

Her tone suggested horrible consequences if the portly guard didn't snap to it. He must have recognized the threat, because he did. Then he backed out of Clarissa's way.

"Uh, you're free to go, mister," he mumbled.

Sam headed down the corridor with Clarissa and David, picked up his personal things in the jail's office, and ducked out the front doors into the bone-jarring Sunday morning sunlight. The instant the doors closed behind them, Clarissa grabbed his arm.

"What was Holly doing with Brad?" she asked, frowning. "We ran into them in the parking lot, but he was hustling her into that gaudy red car of his and we didn't have a chance to talk. What's going on, Sam?"

"Simple. She picked him." Sam shielded his eyes against the sunlight and scanned the parking lot. "Where did you park?"

"Over there." David pointed to their blue Wagoneer, parked at the edge of the lot in the meager shade of a Paloverde tree.

Sam slung his tuxedo jacket over his shoulder and strode over to it. "Would you mind driving me out to the lake? I had to leave my truck there and ride into town with the highway patrolman."

"Sure." David unlocked the driver's-side door, then reached in and unlocked the back door directly behind it.

Sam opened the door and threw in his jacket. He was about to follow it into the back seat when Clarissa grabbed him again. Somehow, she had wedged her body into the space between the back seat, Sam, and the opened door. She scowled at him like a bulldog having a bad day.

"'She picked him.' Is that all you're going to say?" Clarissa demanded.

Sam thought about it. "Yeah."

"Come on, honey," David put in, glancing over his

shoulder at his wife. "Get in. You can badger Sam about his love life on the way to the lake."

"Humph."

Clarissa got in and proceeded to do just that. While David steered the Wagoneer through town toward the highway, she tossed questions at Sam.

"Why was she leaving with Brad? Why didn't Holly just wait for us?" She jabbed her husband. "And how can the two of you act like nothing just happened?" Clarissa paused, fixing them both with a stern look. "Is this a guy thing?"

Sam sighed. "Which question do you want answered first?"

She swiveled in the front seat, straining her shoulder belt to the limit so she could glare at him. "I'm serious. This is a serious thing."

"It's an over-with thing."

Sam looked out his window. They'd hit the interstate, and there was nothing to see except acres of scrubby desert plants, occasionally divided by a sandy arroyo. Sam had grown up here; he couldn't pretend the desert landscape held much interest for him. He turned back to Clarissa.

"Holly didn't wait for you because she didn't know you were coming to bail us out. I didn't tell her. I thought she knew I'd get us out of jail, for Chrissakes! I'm not a total screwup."

His hand fisted against his knee. He wasn't a screwup at all, not anymore. A long time ago Sam had woke up to the fact that he'd been wasting his life away. Wasting his potential away in a haze of parties, women, and the search for a good time. So he'd screwed his head on straighter and found something better.

He was far from perfect, but Sam liked to think he helped most of his students. Once in a while he even came across someone like himself, someone drifting along. Sometimes he gave them a nudge toward bigger goals for themselves, and saw them realize they could do more than they'd thought, after all. Someone like Jiggly Jillian Hall.

"You're not a screwup at all," Clarissa protested. "You're a respected college professor."

"Yeah," David chimed in, "your wild days are behind you, buddy . . . with the obvious exception of today." He grinned into the rearview mirror. "You want to tell us what you were doing naked, with Holly, on some guy's private beach in the middle of the night?"

"No," Sam said flatly. The memory of being with Holly, so close together on the sand, hurt too much to think about. He wouldn't do it.

"I really thought Holly would buckle long before this," Clarissa said, shaking her head. "With Brad out of the picture—and you right there in her house—I thought you were a shoo-in. You seemed like just what Holly needed."

"Honey," David said as he turned down the road leading to Lake Pleasant, "Why do I smell a matchmaking rat in all this? Hmmm?"

Clarissa lifted her chin and gave him a sly smile. "It didn't hurt us any to get thrown together by somebody who cared," she pointed out. She winked at Sam.

He smiled. He was the one who had introduced the two of them—his friend from college, David, and his loud-mouthed cousin, Clarissa. A perfect match. Maybe some kind of matchmaking genes ran in the family.

Sam gave David directions to the landing where they'd parked his truck last night. He picked up his tuxedo jacket and slung it across his lap, seriously considering burning the damn thing. It had brought him nothing but trouble. Since he'd put it on, he and Holly had been kicked out of the formal wear shop and arrested on the beach. For someone like Holly, that was probably too much social censure to swallow all at once.

"Doesn't matter," he said to Clarissa. "Holly got Brad, and I hope she's happy with him."

"No, you don't," Clarissa said. "You hope they're miserable together and she comes back to you. Admit it."

So what if he did? It wasn't going to happen.

"They belong together. They're perfectly well suited for one another."

"Oh, jeez—now Holly's got you believing that junk, too? David, she's brainwashed him. We've got to do something."

Clarissa smacked the back of the seat with her hand, looking exasperated. "Hello? Sam? You don't fall in love with somebody because you share shoe sizes and an interest in Keogh accounts."

David pulled up to the left of Sam's truck, crunching gravel beneath his tires and spitting it against the underbody of his Wagoneer. The whole vehicle swayed on the pitted ground, then stopped.

Sam opened his door. "You're preaching to the converted," he told Clarissa. "Thanks for the ride."

"Wait a minute!"

Clarissa jumped out of the Wagoneer right behind him, and hustled to meet Sam beside his truck. She leaned against the driver's-side door, arms crossed.

"You're not going anywhere until I get some answers."

"Oh, yeah?" Sam caught hold of her upper arms, lifted her a few inches above the sandy ground, and set her down out of his way. He unlocked his truck door.

"That's not fair! I'm only here because I care about you, and you know it."

He cracked open his door, then faced her. "I'm tired," he said gently. "I'm dead tired and a little pissed-off and a lot sick of talking about this. It feels like my heart got stuck in a vise and twisted like hell. So cut me a little slack, okay? We can talk about this when I get back."

Clarissa came closer and wrapped her arms around his middle.

"I'm sorry," she said, laying her head against his chest. "I'm so sorry things worked out like this, and—"

Her head rose sharply and she released him. "And did you just say we'll talk about it when you get back? Back from where? Where are you going?"

"I've got to get away."

Sam climbed into his truck. Inside it still smelled like Holly's flowery perfume; her lipstick tube was still tucked into the passenger-side visor where she'd left it before the party. He gripped the steering wheel tighter. There was no way in hell Sam was going back to her house and watch her rebuild things with Brad.

Goodbye, Sam . . . I'm sorry things had to end this way.

He was sorry, too. Sorry things had ever begun, only to

turn sour at the end. Sam shoved his keys into the ignition and started his truck. The sooner he left, the better.

"Sam, where are you going?"

"Back to Tucson. I've got to be there anyway—my ethics hearing is scheduled later this week. Remember Malcolm's charges, about changing Jilly's grade?"

Clarissa nodded. "Malcolm's a worm. You can tell him that for me when you see him." She grinned, looking cheered by the thought.

"After that . . . I don't know." Sam shrugged. "Maybe I'll set up a late-session summer school class to teach. Take my mind off things."

"I don't think you should go, Sam," Clarissa said unhappily.

"I can't stay here." He pulled the truck door closed and rolled down the window. He drummed his fingers on the edge of it, needing to be gone. Needing to forget.

She sighed. "I know. What should I tell Holly?"

Sam's heart twisted again. "Tell her . . . tell her if she decides to take a chance, I'll be waiting. Tell her love at first sight is real." He paused. "Tell her I still believe that fortune cookie was right."

"Huh?" Clarissa looked puzzled.

"She'll know what it means." Sam put his truck into gear. "I'll let you know where I wind up."

"Wait—you want me to tell her about a fortune cookie?"

He looked at her. Why was he still hoping?

"On second thought," Sam said, "just tell her I said goodbye."

He pulled out of the landing and onto the highway, and pretty soon Sam was making good time toward Tucson—the direction exactly opposite of the one he really wanted to go.

Just after sunset, Brad took Holly home. As they pulled into her driveway, she peered out at the darkened windows of her house and knew things really were finished between her and Sam. He wasn't there.

Holly's heart sank. Part of her had been hoping, admittedly without reason, that Sam would be waiting for her. Beside her, Brad cut the BMW's engine and stretched his arm across the back of her seat, looking satisfied with himself.

"I'm certainly glad I didn't hire an outside consultant to evaluate that accounting software for me. It would have cost me a bundle."

It was as close as Brad would come to a thank you. Somehow, he'd persuaded her to look over his new software package for him after all. Holly had spent the whole afternoon in his office setting up portions of it for him.

"I'm glad I could help," she said.

She shifted uncomfortably in the car's leather upholstered seat, feeling awkward and overdressed in the beige seersucker dress and matching jacket Brad had bought for her earlier. The clothes had been waiting in the car when they'd left the jail. He'd insisted on taking her to his new, luxurious condominium to shower and change before heading to his office.

Brad's condominium had all the warmth of a modern-art museum. It was all slick surfaces and cold, hard edges. Even the landscaping outside was cold, a mixture of granite boulders accented with knifelike desert Agave. Holly hadn't wanted to admit how well its austerity suited him.

"Do you want to come inside?" Holly asked, nodding toward her dark, empty-looking house. "The renovation is practically finished. It looks nice—I'd like you to see it."

Brad shook his head. "No, thanks. I've had enough reminders of your friend Sam's handiwork for one day."

She looked away, remembering all the times she'd mentioned Sam's name. So many things reminded her of him. Holly hadn't realized how much those references might hurt Brad.

"I'm sorry, Brad—I'm sure that won't happen again."

"I hope not. The guy was ruining your reputation, getting you thrown out of stores—getting you arrested!" He pursed his lips. "I'm afraid your exploits didn't do my reputation any favors, either. Everyone in town still associates us together, you know."

Brad reached into the back seat and retrieved her white party dress, newly cleaned and wrapped in a dry cleaner's bag. Still holding it, he opened his car door and got out.

Holly watched him walk around the front of the car. He paused, wiped a spot from the hood with his sleeve, then came around to her side and opened her door. "I'll walk you up to your door, though," he offered with a smile.

She let him help her out of the car—always a gentleman, Brad was—and walk her to the front porch. He spread her dress across the porch swing.

"I understand about Sam, though," he said, facing her again. "Actually, I admire your quick thinking. It was a good way to get your renovation done cheaply."

"It wasn't like that. Sam was . . . a friend." A friend and more, someone who'd always thought of her happiness. How could Brad make their relationship sound so mercenary?

Brad waved away her explanation. "It doesn't matter anyway. Luckily for you, your little plan finally worked."

He spread his arms wide, an odd sort of smirk on his handsome face. She couldn't read his expression very well, because he still had his sunglasses on, even though it was getting dark. "You got me."

"What?"

"You got me. You got what you wanted, with your plan. *The* plan. It was all there in your day planner."

"You read my day planner?" Holly grabbed the top of the waist-high porch wall and leaned against it. She needed the support.

Moving closer, Brad frowned. "Only by accident. I saw my name on some of the pages, and naturally I was curious." Trying to lighten the mood, he added, "Once I got going, though, it was quite a read."

"You had no right. That was private."

Holly had thought being unceremoniously dumped on the night of the romantic dinner that wasn't was bad. She'd thought being ridiculed and then ignored on the golf course was bad. She'd thought being turned down while dressed in her most seductive clothes was bad. This was worse.

"And now you're making fun of me because of something you read while you were snooping?" she asked, her voice growing louder.

Holly had a horrible thought—how long ago had he read about her plan? Had he known, almost from the start, what she was doing? The idea was humiliating.

"It was really very flattering. What man could resist being the subject of such—"

"When did you read it?" Holly interrupted. She pushed away from the porch wall to confront him. "When?"

"I don't see what you're getting so upset about. It was just a stupid little thing—"

She snatched Brad's damned black sunglasses from his face so she could look him in the eye, and straightened to her full height. Wearing her heels, Holly had a good two inches on him. For once, it felt good.

"When?"

Brad blinked nervously, his face pale and somehow diminished without the glasses he always wore. "This morning. While you were in the shower."

Holly fought the urge to whip off her spike-heeled shoe and hurl it at him. *"Why?"*

"I wanted your mother's phone number at her real estate office." He glared at her, as though she were being completely unreasonable. "I called to find out how much we might get for your house. To find out if she'd list it for sale with her agency."

Brad snatched back his sunglasses. Feeling stunned, Holly stepped away from him and sank onto the porch swing. Her dress, still in its dry cleaner's bag, crinkled beneath her. She didn't have the energy to care.

"You know I always hated this old house, Holly," Brad went on. "We should start fresh, start over in a new place— like my condo. Now that we're together again—"

"No."

"Huh?"

"No." Oh, Lord—she'd been such a fool. How could she have been so blind?

She'd been so afraid to be a failure. So afraid of winding up alone. So certain the problems in their relationship could be—should be—fixed, if only she tried hard enough.

Holly shook her head. "No, Brad. We're not together—I'm not sure we ever were." She looked up at him, picking up speed as she went on talking. "I tried everything to make things work between us. Everything. And you know what I just realized?"

Brad cautiously shook his head. He was probably still reeling from the realization that he wasn't taller than Holly after all.

"It's not my fault."

It was true. Her Plan should've worked, probably would've worked—on anyone who really cared for her. Anyone except Brad the Bad. Holly wasn't the failure in their relationship—Brad was. Realizing the truth of that was like a shot of pure sunshine to her battered spirit.

It wasn't Holly's Plan that had won him back. Her Plan was only one big, ego-stroking joke to him. Brad's need to save his own reputation made him come back—not to mention his need for a part-time accountant. Holly narrowed her eyes at him. She'd gotten what she wanted, all right—only to find out it wasn't worth having.

"I think you should leave, Brad."

"Come on," he said, giving her his most charming smile, "don't make more of this than it really is. You said yourself we belong together."

Holly stood and gathered up her dress. "Not anymore," she said. "Frankly, I'd rather be alone."

He stared at her. "You will be alone," he snarled. "Even your handyman's gone, thanks to the kiss-off you gave him at the jail this morning. And you won't get a second chance with me, not this time."

Brad turned, so mad he clomped awkwardly down the steps. On the sidewalk, he turned to her. "How does it feel to be unwanted?" he asked snidely.

She didn't want to hurt him. She really didn't. Holly looked at him for a long moment.

"Maybe you should ask yourself that question," she said

quietly. Then she turned, unlocked the door, and slipped inside. Alone.

"You're crazy," Clarissa said a few days later. She plopped into the floral-upholstered armchair beside Holly's newly repaired fireplace and stared into the fire. Then she looked up at Holly again.

"You've got a man who loves you,"—she leaned forward—"Sam, in case you're wondering—and you're letting him get away."

"He's already gone," Holly muttered glumly, poking at the fire.

She'd never been able to use the fireplace before. She'd never even seen it when it wasn't boarded up. Maybe she shouldn't be using it now, either—it was almost a hundred and ten degrees outside. They'd had to turn the air-conditioning to sixty-two degrees to avoid bringing heat exhaustion on themselves.

It made Holly feel closer to Sam to use the fireplace, though. It was absurd, she knew. But she had the same kind of cozy feeling whenever she used the new porcelain sink he'd installed in the kitchen. Holly felt it when she hung pictures on the freshly painted walls, and she felt it when she stepped onto the new hardwood kitchen floor instead of the old yellow linoleum.

She missed him.

"He's only gone because he thinks you chose Brad," Clarissa insisted for what had to be the hundredth time. "Call him. I gave you the number."

Holly shook her head. "I can't. What if Sam doesn't want me anymore? What if he hates me? I couldn't stand it if I called him and he hated me."

She replaced the wrought-iron fireplace poker in its holder and sat on the sofa. In the corner were the pink-fringed throw pillows she'd used to prop up Sam's injured foot. Reminders of him were everywhere. Holly picked one up and hugged it in her lap.

"I still have my memories. At least this way I can still

dream of what might have happened." She shuddered. "I don't want to know the truth. I was so mean to him at the end. How could Sam ever forgive me?"

"You're right. He never will," Clarissa deadpanned. "He's probably sticking pins in a Holly Aldridge voodoo doll right now. He's probably telling total strangers how lucky he was to get away from you."

Holly covered her face with the pillow. Clarissa was probably right. She felt horrible.

"You know, I even ordered Kung Pao Chicken last night. And a pizza from Angelo's the night before," Holly said forlornly, her voice muffled by the pillow. She looked up. "It wasn't the same without Sam."

She'd taken to sleeping in Sam's bed in the guest bedroom, too. Worse, Holly hadn't even changed the sheets first. She imagined they smelled vaguely, but wonderfully, like Sam. She was turning into a real basket case.

Clarissa shrieked. "I was *kidding!* Jeez, get it through your head, Holly. Sam—loves—you. He's not going to stop. You should've seen his face when he left."

Lowering the pillow slightly, Holly peeped, "Really?"

Clarissa threw her hands in the air. *"Yes.* What do you think I've been trying to pound into that thick head of yours for the past three days?"

"I still can't call him. I just can't take a chance like that."

"Do it."

Holly shook her head. "I can't."

"You can. Do it."

Trying to ignore her friend, Holly pulled a fresh tissue from the supply she'd taken to keeping in her pocket, and blew her nose.

"You know, I haven't even been in to work since last Friday," she admitted.

"I know—I work there too, remember?" Clarissa gave her a sympathetic look. "Anyway, you've probably accrued about a thousand sick days. You deserve it."

She got up and sat beside Holly on the couch, then gave her a hug. "That only proves my point, hon. For you, missing work is like breaking the law."

SURRENDER

Holly sniffled. Clarissa had a point. This was serious.

"This is a chance you can't afford *not* to take," Clarissa said. "Isn't true love worth it?"

Holly took a deep, quavery breath and spoke aloud her greatest fear. "What if Sam doesn't want me anymore?"

Clarissa looked solemnly at her, then gave her a squeeze. "There's only one way to find out," she said.

"You sure about this?" Sam's landlord asked him, pushing the lease agreement across the kitchen table for Sam to sign.

"Yeah." He scanned the document, then scrawled his name at the bottom and handed it over. It was a done deal.

Beside him sat Jiggly Jillian Hall. Her two toddlers—a boy and a girl, both with identical curly, pale blond hair—played noisily in his apartment living room. He could hear their toys banging, and the sound of their babyish laughter.

"I hope they won't break anything," Jillie said, giving him a worried look.

"Nah," Sam replied with a wink at his landlord, "the furniture comes with the place, and I'm sure it's been through worse. It would take a jackhammer to make a dent in any of it."

"Hey, you're making me look bad," his landlord protested. "There's nothing wrong with that stuff." He peered semisuspiciously at Sam. "You sure about this deal? Maybe you're having second thoughts about losing a nice, cheap apartment like this."

"I already told you, I'm not." Sam got up and shook hands with his landlord. "Thanks for everything. Just don't go raising the rent on Jillie, here. She's got a lease, remember?"

"Yeah, okay." His landlord picked up the lease, took a copy for himself, and headed for the front door. He was still muttering something about "never had no kids here before," when he left. Sam didn't think it would be a problem. The day he'd first moved in, the landlord had gone on at length about "never had no college students here before."

Besides, Sam had already overhead him telling Jillie what

nice little rugrats she had. Despite his bluster, the guy was a softie at heart.

Sam picked up his last moving box and went into the living room to say goodbye to the kids. Jillie followed him.

"It's a great place," he told her. "I hope you'll be happy here. With two bedrooms, it was always too big for me, anyway."

She smiled. "Oh, we will be, professor! The kids never had their own room before. They'll be just tickled."

Jillie looked pretty happy herself. Sam grinned back at her. The movement felt strange—he hadn't been feeling much like smiling lately. Losing Holly made everything look gray.

He wished Jillie good luck and they said their goodbyes, then he hefted the box again and carried it outside to his truck. Sam shoved it in place atop the rest and tied the whole mess down. He'd be on his way in no time.

Honk! Honk! Sam turned at the sound, shading his eyes to peer down the street. A little white convertible, horn blaring with as much enthusiasm as its tiny size could muster, zoomed straight toward him. Holly was at the wheel.

Holly was going to run him down, judging by the speed she was traveling. Maybe three days with Brad had sent her over the edge. Sam figured a guy like Brad could do that to a person.

She wrenched the car to a gravel-crunching stop a few feet away and leapt out without opening the door. Sam rubbed his eyes. He had to be hallucinating. Either that, or dreaming. Holly had way too much decorum to jump out of a car, especially when she was wearing that sexy white dress of hers—which she was.

"Sam!"

"Holly?"

"I can't believe I found you." She threw herself into his arms and clamped herself onto him so tightly it would take a crowbar to pry her away. She was real, all right. Sam would've recognized the feel of Holly in his arms no matter how it happened.

"I drove straight here," she said, the words rushing out,

"but I went to the University first and you weren't there. So then I went looking for your apartment, but I got lost. I was driving around in circles and then I saw your truck and here I am."

Holly paused for breath, then plunged ahead. He couldn't get a word in edgewise. "Sam, Brad and I are through. For good, this time. I was a complete idiot. Can you forgive me? Please forgive me, I'm so sorry for everything."

Holly stopped and looked at his truck bed, piled high with moving boxes and the rest of his things. "Where are you going?" she asked, her expression turning serious.

"I—"

"Is it because of me? Were you trying to get away before I got here? You were, weren't you? I'll *kill* Clarissa if she's the one who called you."

She sagged in his arms, close to tears, looking desolate. And gorgeous. And like everything he'd ever wanted. Sam pulled Holly close and kissed her. When he raised his head again, she looked slightly dazed. Sam took advantage of the opportunity to explain.

"Clarissa didn't call me," Sam said. "I—"

Holly gasped. "Oh, no—you lost your ethics hearing, didn't you? I can't believe it, those—"

She squinted, probably trying to think up something really vile to call the university faculty. Sam grinned down at her.

"No, I didn't lose. In fact, Malcolm's ridiculous charge got thrown out—laughed out, more like it."

In fact, it hadn't even reached the stage of a formal ethics hearing, but between his moves from Tucson to his parent's house and then to Holly's, the notices hadn't reached him. Sam hadn't found out about it until he arrived.

"I quit," he went on. Her eyes widened. "I took another job," he explained, "one where I wouldn't have to deal with somebody like Malcolm Jeffries. Life's too short to spend your days working with a jerk like him."

"Oh."

"What, no lecture about job responsibilities? No warnings about the dangers of unemployment? No speeches about the necessity of planning ahead?" Sam put a hand to her forehead. "Are you sure you're feeling all right?"

They both laughed.

"I'm feeling fine," Holly said, all but purring with the certainty of her statement. "And you don't need a plan, because I've already got one for both of us."

"You do?" He kissed her shoulder, then her neck.

"Yes."

She pressed a slip of paper into his hand, folding his fingers tightly around it. "You were right all along," Holly said. "I was falling in love with you. I was just too stubborn and too dumb to admit it."

Sam unfolded the paper. In his hand was the fortune-cookie fortune from their Kung Pao Chicken dinner. *Your present plans are going to succeed.*

"I love you, Sam," she whispered. "And I never want to lose you again."

He held her close, his lips against her hair. "You never will," Sam said. He considered turning a few happy cartwheels on the lawn, then dismissed the idea. He'd have to let Holly go in order to do that. "God, I missed you. There's no way I'll lose you again."

"Well," she said, sounding businesslike despite the fact that her face was squashed against his chest, "I want to make sure."

Holly stepped back and took a deep breath. "Marry me. I've already got the dress, see?"

She held out both hands and turned in a circle. "You said it was perfect for a wedding dress."

"Wow. When you make a decision, you really take it all the way," Sam said, admiring the woman he loved.

"I don't like to do things halfway." She smiled. "Is that a yes?"

Sam picked up Holly and twirled her around in a circle, and now he was smiling, too. "Yes. Yes, yes, yes, yes, yes."

Chapter Eleven

It was going to be a perfectly romantic evening. The lighting was soft, the music was seductive, the wine was cold. Even the weather had cooperated, in the form of a late-summer Arizona rainstorm that thrummed on the roof with a hypnotic rhythm. It was the kind of night that invited snuggling up in front of a toasty fire and forgetting the rest of the world existed.

Things started going uphill from the moment Holly's husband Sam came home from his new teaching job at the community college. He came in the door, dripping rainwater from the bunch of black-eyed Susans in his hand. Juggling the flowers, Sam shucked off his shoes, stripped off his wet suit jacket, his tie, and his shirt, and came toward her in the darkness.

"Power go out?" he asked.

"Nooo," Holly said, smiling. She patted the sofa cushion.

Sam reached the sofa and dropped the flowers on the coffee table. "I'm kidding," he said. "I recognize a romantic evening when I see one."

Gently, he pushed her back on the sofa. His fingers

delved into her hair, stroking. His mouth found Holly's, and his strong, hard body settled comfortably against hers.

"Where's the pizza from Angelo's?" he asked, grinning. "You can't perform a cheap pizza-and-wine seduction routine without it. I'm not easy, you know."

Holly rubbed her cheek against his, then she nuzzled his neck. She loved him more every day. "It's in the kitchen," she murmured, "but I've got other plans for you. And they're happening right here."

"I love it already," Sam said, bringing her close for another kiss.

As romantic evenings went, Holly thought, this one was starting out . . . perfectly. She had a feeling it would end that way, too—happily ever after.